Slowly, Harry moved her away from him, his eyes ablaze with a peculiar light. 'Would you say a kiss like that means something?'

Lisa wished the ground would swallow her up. 'Why are you doing this?'

'To show you the dangers of reading too much into things. It's still a mistake to get entangled with me. I thought you understood.'

She scrubbed her mouth with the back of her hand. 'You're a bastard, Harry.'

'Shall I put it in writing?'

'There's no need. I doubt if I'll forget again as long as I live.' She *had* been reading too much into their situation, hoping that this time things would be different between them. She almost wished she had taken her chances with Tyler Thornton on the cruise. Whatever had made her think she would be safer with Harry Blake?

ISLAND
OF DREAMS

BY

VALERIE PARV

MILLS & BOON LIMITED
ETON HOUSE   18-24 PARADISE ROAD
RICHMOND   SURREY   TW9 1SR

First published in Great Britain 1992
by Mills & Boon Limited

© Valerie Parv 1992

Australian copyright 1992
Philippine copyright 1992
This edition 1992

ISBN 0 263 77411 2

Set in Times Roman 11 on 12 pt.
92-9204-46103 C

Made and printed in Great Britain

CHAPTER ONE

LISA ALEXANDER tapped her pen against her teeth. She should take notes, but it was much easier to lose herself in the easy, uncomplicated beauty of Thursday Island. The oven-like heat, the cobalt and sapphire colours of the ocean, and a pearling lugger riding at anchor, looked more like a scene from *South Pacific* than a potential tourist destination at the northernmost tip of Australia.

In the distance the islands of the Torres Strait floated in a haze of blue on blue while the golden blaze of the sun sparked diamond points of light off the azure waves.

Lisa sighed. How did a granddaughter of the Russian steppes get to be so lucky? But for her parents' life-changing decision, made the year she was born, she could have been surveying the travel possibilities in Vladivostock instead of tropical Australia.

Suddenly a figure crossed her line of vision and she tensed as every nerve-ending in her body shrilled a silent protest. Unwillingly her lips formed his name. Harry Blake.

From this distance she couldn't see his face, but there was no mistaking his lean, muscular shape which gave an impression of tallness although he was only an inch or so taller than herself. Spare, almost triangular in shape, he had wide shoulders, tapering to a narrow waist and hips. One shoulder was slightly higher than the other, the result of a sporting accident in his youth. When she had last seen him a superbly cut business suit had disguised the slight flaw. His present khaki work clothes concealed nothing. Open-throated, his shirt revealed dark hair V-ing downwards, while his moleskin trousers rode low on his hips, held in place by a dark leather belt angled as rakishly as a cowboy's gunbelt.

Her throat dried with more than the tropical heat. She had resigned herself to never seeing Harry Blake again. Unprepared, she reeled from the shock of the unexpected encounter. What was he doing on Thursday Island?

An instinctive reaction had driven her into the shade of a wongai tree and she backed against it, her brain whirling. Once she would have raced forward without a second thought, flinging herself into his arms with a cry of greeting. But she wasn't nineteen any more, and even then Harry hadn't welcomed her affection. She chewed her lower lip, wishing she had the courage to walk up and shake his hand as if they were merely old acquaintances meeting by chance.

'Fancy running into you here,' she would say, her tone cool and composed.

His husky reply echoed in her imagination. 'Well, if it isn't little Lisanko Nikitayevna Alexandrov.'

He had always teased her about her full name. 'It's simply Lisa Alexander these days,' she would reply. 'And I'm not so little any more.'

She allowed herself to imagine how his grey eyes would rove over her olive limbs as the wind whipped the cotton sundress against the slender outlines of her legs. A white leather belt cinched the dress in at her waist, accentuating the swell of her breasts. Her figure was no accident, having been honed by careful diet and hours of aerobics classes. Would he notice the change?

Her colour heightened as she remembered him poking a teasing finger into the soft teenage flesh above her waist. 'Too many *piroshkis*,' he had said. She had laughed, but had foresworn her mother's rich Russian cooking ever afterwards. At nineteen such comments tended to sting.

Puppy-fat and puppy-love. She had shed one and was fairly sure she had buried the other. So why did the sight of Harry Blake now, when she was a mature career woman of twenty-four, set her pulses racing and her heart hammering in her chest?

While she'd wrestled with her memories he had walked on and now leaned against a railing, staring out to sea. If she retraced her steps back to town he would never know she had glimpsed him. She swung around, tempted to put the thought into action. Her business with Harry was finished a long time ago.

A movement behind her caught her eye and she suppressed a groan. The Torres Strait islands boasted a population of four thousand people at best. The odds against meeting any two individuals here were astronomical. But not only was Harry Blake here, but behind her was Tyler Thornton, the journalist she had come to Cape York to avoid. She was still in shadow, but if he continued on his purposeful way he would spot her in seconds.

The phrase 'caught between a rock and a hard place' sprang to mind as her head swivelled between the two men. Which one was the lesser of two evils?

Her feet made the decision for her. Before she fully realised what she meant to do she found herself closing the gap between herself and Harry.

All the glib phrases she might have used deserted her as she reached for his arm. 'Harry, it *is* you.'

As he turned to her his grey eyes softened. For all the surprise he showed, he could have been waiting for her. 'Hello, Lisa.'

She risked a glance over her shoulder. Tyler Thornton's steps had faltered and he stood under the tree, watching them warily. 'I need a favour,' she told Harry softly.

'Name it.'

'There's a man following me and I'd rather not have to speak to him.'

His head never lifted but his eyes flickered to the man behind them and back to her face again. 'Tyler Thornton?'

'Do you know him?'

'I know him.' The disgust in his voice told his own story. 'We worked for the same newspaper years ago.'

'He's hounding me about a story. I've told him I can't help him, but he won't leave me alone.'

'Then it's time Mr Thornton learned how to take no for an answer.'

To Lisa's consternation, Harry's arm slid around her shoulders and he pulled her to him, his lips brushing her hairline in an affectionate gesture.

She tensed. 'What are you doing?'

'Putting on a show for our audience.'

So that was all he was doing—convincing Tyler Thornton that this was a deliberate meeting. Knowing it was an act didn't stop her senses flaring into overdrive, until she forced herself to relax. 'Is this better?'

'Much better.' Keeping his head close to hers, he steered her away from where Thornton stood, and back in the direction of the town.

Arm in arm, they walked along the main street. As they turned a corner Lisa glimpsed Thornton watching them open-mouthed. He hadn't counted on her having a protector on the island.

Protector or predator? All of a sudden she realised what she had done. She might have known Harry well when she was a teenager and he'd practically lived with her family, but she hadn't seen him in over five years. People changed, and she had virtually thrown herself into his arms.

He felt the shudder which rippled through her. 'It's all right; you're safe with me. Safer than with Thornton, at any rate.'

She ignored the *frisson* of excitement which followed the shudder, refusing to recognise it as a product of Harry's closeness. It was the unexpectedness of finding herself in his arms which made her skin feel electrified. Her feelings for him were dead and buried by Harry himself, so it couldn't be anything else.

'Here we are,' he said into her ear.

He opened a door, standing aside to let her precede him. She found herself confronted by a circle of black faces regarding her with friendly curiosity. They were in a pub which a tour guide had pointed out to her earlier. It was a favourite haunt of the island's Aboriginal people.

Disconcerted, she looked at Harry. 'Won't they mind our coming in here?'

He grinned at a black man leaning against the bar. 'Will you mind if we come in here, Dan?'

The man smiled back. 'I'll mind like hell, Harry. Lowers the tone of the place.' He switched his gaze to Lisa and nodded his approval. 'Now the lady's another matter. She adds a bit of class.'

'Sorry, we're a matched set,' Harry said evenly. He steered her through the room, exchanging greetings as they went, until they emerged into a beer garden shaded by lush palm-trees and thickets of bamboo. 'Wait here. I want a word with Dan, then I'll bring you a cold drink.'

Through a set of glass doors she saw him approach Dan and gesture towards the street entrance. Dan nodded and raised his glass in salute. A few minutes later Harry returned, carrying a large glass of amber liquid and a smaller one which he set in front of her. 'I got you a shandy. Is that all right?'

The combination of beer and lemonade was a welcome thirst-quencher in the tropics, where she knew better than to order fancy cocktails. 'Perfect,' she said, raising the glass to her parched lips. The foaming liquid cooled her throat and she cupped her hands around the dewy glass, enjoying its chill feel against her fiery skin.

Suddenly a commotion erupted in the bar behind them. Startled, she looked up to see Dan and another man apparently engaged in an all-in brawl. There was a lot of scuffling and swearing, and dust rose in a cloud around them. The street door opened and Tyler Thornton appeared on the threshold.

Harry had chosen their table carefully, she saw now. From where they sat they could see everything happening inside, while being screened from view themselves by the trees.

'What's going on?' she asked, unnerved by the sudden eruption into violence.

Harry sipped his beer calmly. 'Nothing to worry about. But I don't think Thornton will stick around long, do you?'

Understanding dawned and her eyes widened. 'You asked Dan to stage a brawl to put Thornton off coming here?'

'Not exactly. I only said we needed a little privacy.'

'Very resourceful, your Dan,' she murmured, nonplussed by Harry's idea of a diversion. It was working, she saw, as Tyler rapidly withdrew and the door swung shut behind him. Instantly the combatants dusted themselves off and went back to their beers, laughing and slapping each other on the backs. One of them gave Harry a thumbs-up sign which he returned.

'You did all that for me?' she asked, bemused.

'What else are friends for?' His shoulders lifted in an uneven but eloquent shrug. 'Now suppose you start at the beginning.'

She hesitated. He had been very good about helping her to evade Tyler Thornton, but she had no right to intrude on his life. 'You needn't concern yourself with me any more,' she demurred. 'It was the greatest luck running into you here and you've been wonderful, but Thornton has given up now, so——'

'People like him never give up,' he cut across her, his tone harsh. 'And our meeting wasn't exactly due to luck.'

She stared at him. 'How can it be anything else? I only found out I was coming to Cape York last week.'

'To check out a new cruise between Thursday Island and Cairns,' he supplied. At her startled reaction amusement flickered across his features. 'Who do you think persuaded the cruise people to invite you?'

'You? But how? Why?' She was stammering foolishly but the idea of Harry Blake engineering her visit here was too astonishing for words. She'd thought he never wanted to see her again.

He took a long drink of his beer, and foam flecked his upper lip until he licked it away. Her own mouth felt arid as she observed the movement and she clenched her hands under the table, shocked by the intensity of her feelings.

'The how is easy. The skipper of *Reef Lady* is a friend of mine,' he explained. 'Through my newspaper connections I got a tip-off that Thornton was after you, so I decided to do what I could to help.'

'So you arranged for my travel agency to send me here to pick up the cruise,' she concluded, and his nod confirmed it. 'That only leaves the why.'

He raked long fingers through the blue-black waves of his hair. 'It's no mystery, either. I know you're alone since losing your folks last year. It was the least I could do for the daughter of a good friend.'

Despite the tropical heat, a chill settled on her spine. He was only returning a favour to her father. For a moment she'd thought...no, she should have known better. Harry Blake had no time for her, a fact he'd made abundantly clear when she'd made the mistake of falling in love with him just before her nineteenth birthday. After shattering her illusions he had disappeared from her life. Their only contact since he'd finished writing her father's life story had been a letter of condolence after her parents had died.

'I was sorry about what happened,' he said.

'I know.' She nodded without looking up. She still felt her loss acutely. His note had been the one bright spot in that blackest of weeks after her parents were killed when their fishing boat caught fire not far from Cairns.

She'd waited and hoped for more contact from him but nothing had come. 'If you were so concerned for my welfare you could have gotten in touch,' she said sharply.

'Until now I've had no reason to.'

'You could have written or called to see how I . . . how we were getting along.'

He didn't appear to notice her slip of the tongue. 'I knew how you were getting along. Nick wrote to me regularly until he died.'

This was news to her. 'Papa never mentioned your letters.'

'I asked him not to. I always admired your father, Lisa. Not many men have the courage of their convictions as he did.'

She knew he was referring to her father's defection from Russia with his pregnant wife, Marya, so that their child could be born in the freedom of the West. 'I know. I miss him terribly. I tell myself his last years were good ones. He really liked working for Cairns City Council and fishing in his spare time.'

'It's a long way from his first trip outside Russia, working on the Aswân Dam.'

She smiled. 'He used to say it was all engineering, and if it made people's lives more comfortable . . .' She tailed off on a shrug which betrayed her Tartar heritage. 'I'm just glad he and Mama are together.'

'She couldn't have gone on without him.'

Lisa nodded. How well he knew her parents. 'Mama never adjusted to life in the West. She was so self-conscious about her Russian accent that she never socialised. The publicity surrounding your book was agony for her.'

Harry looked thoughtful. 'Yet your father went ahead with the project anyway.'

'She wanted him to. They both hated the lies and distortions which were written about the family when we came to Australia. They wanted their story told accurately, and that series of articles you wrote about immigrants to Australia convinced them they could trust you.'

' "Strangers in a Strange Land",' he echoed, recalling the title of the series. 'It collected a swag of awards, but most of all it enabled your father to trust me. His life-story inspired many people.'

She smiled, remembering. 'I don't think he expected it to have such an impact, far less be sold to Hollywood.'

Harry's grimace matched hers. 'I'm only sorry we had no control over the film once the rights were sold. *Divided Hearts* remains one of my favourite books.'

'I still have my autographed copy,' she said. 'You wrote, "To Lisanko, may you never have to choose between two loves".'

'Sentimental old fool,' he growled.

Something sharp pierced her core. She did a quick mental calculation. 'Thirty-two isn't so old. You make yourself sound grizzled and ancient.'

'Maybe it's how I feel,' he said dismissively.

They were interrupted by a massively built black man wearing an apron tied under his arms over denim work-clothes. In each hand he balanced a plate, setting one in front of each of them. 'Enjoy your lunch, folks.'

Harry paid him. 'Thanks, Gunner.'

As the man left she raised her eyebrows. 'Gunner?'

'The locals named him for all the things he's "gunner" do one of these days.'

She laughed but the sound faded as she regarded the food in front of her. Beside an enormous hamburger was a small mountain of fried potatoes.

In front of Harry was a real seashell containing green salad topped by fresh prawns still in their shells. Harry saw her disappointed expression. 'Is something wrong with your lunch?'

'Why did you order a hamburger for me and seafood for yourself?'

'You prefer that kind of thing. You used to love junk food.'

Her eyes swam and she blinked hard. Was he so blind that he couldn't see how much she'd changed? 'I was growing up then,' she defended herself.

'And growing out,' he agreed. 'I've never known anyone who liked their tucker as much as you did, Lisa.'

It was true. As a teenager she had been obsessed with food until counselling had helped her to understand the reason. She now knew that her problems stemmed from growing up in an atmosphere of insecurity, moving house time after time until her parents had finally accepted that no one was going to force them back to their homeland. With little chance to make friends normally it was no wonder that she had turned to food as consolation.

Angrily she pushed the plate away. 'Don't worry, I'll pay for the food, so you haven't wasted your money.'

His hand clamped over her wrist, stemming her flight. 'Never mind the money. What's the matter, Lisa?'

She ignored the heat flaring along her arm at his touch. 'Good old Harry Blake, always so sensitive to my feelings. It seems you haven't changed.'

'All I did was order lunch, for goodness' sake. If it offends your women's lib principles I'm sorry.' But his tone held no hint of real apology.

Her eyes misted and she blinked furiously. 'Women's liberation has nothing to do with it. It's your high-handed assumption that you know what's best for me, when you don't.' And never did, she added in silent fury.

As if emerging from a trance he released her and looked at her, really looked for the first time since she'd approached him on the waterfront.

Behind him was a mirror on the wall and she tried to see herself in it, through his eyes. Her glossy black hair flowed to her shoulders, held back from her face by tortoiseshell combs. Her dull gold skin was stained with red, both from the sun and her recent outburst. The effect emphasised her high Slavic cheekbones. And right now the light of battle flickered in her amber eyes. There was a world of difference between herself at nineteen and what the mirror showed now.

Her gaze shifted to his face. He had changed, too, but in subtle ways. His features were more rugged than she remembered, the cleft in his chin deeper, tempting her to touch it to see if it were a trick of the light. His mouth still possessed a slightly arrogant cut which was somehow exciting, and faint hollows under his cheekbones suggested that his life to date held its share of sadness.

His grey eyes were veiled by the sweep of his long lashes which curled slightly on to his cheeks. Then they lifted and she grew hot as she realised he was laughing at her.

He forestalled her yet again. 'You're right, you have changed,' he agreed. 'Your temper is much hotter than I remember.'

Was that all he noticed about her? She subsided in her seat, wondering where this sick feeling of disappointment came from. Surely she didn't expect compliments from him? Last time he had barely acknowledged that she was female.

To her surprise he pushed the plate of seafood towards her and lifted the hamburger on to his side of the table. 'Now will you stay and have lunch with me?'

It was hardly a gallant invitation but she found herself wanting to accept. 'This looks very nice,' she said a little primly.

'Another drink?'

She nodded and he went to fetch them. When he came back she was inordinately pleased to see that he had brought Diet Pepsi for them both. The ice clinked in the glasses as he set them down. They ate in silence for a while, then Harry asked, 'How did you get entangled with the likes of Tyler Thornton?'

She paused in the act of shelling a succulent prawn. 'He approached me. I thought, with my parents gone, the media would lose interest, but it flared up as a result of the accident. Nostalgia pieces popped up everywhere.'

Harry nodded sympathetically. 'I saw some of them.'

A shudder shook her. 'Those baby pictures of me—ugh! But there was no scandal, no big inheritance, so after a while it all died down again.'

'Then along comes Thornton, following a lead of his own.'

She rested her chin on one hand. 'Does he make a habit of digging for his stories in people's pasts?'

'Mostly in the dirt.'

'In my case there isn't any. He insists my parents left a photo, which he's hounding me to let him publish.'

'And did they?'

'Not that I know of. At least, it wasn't among their things. Not that they left very much,' she added wistfully. 'They brought so little with them out of Russia. About the only photo they had is their wedding picture and I've checked it with a magnifying glass. There's nothing in it to interest the media.'

'Did he tell you what's supposed to be in the photo?'

She traced a line across the table's scarred timber surface. 'He hasn't had much chance. When he calls at home he gets my answering machine, and at work Simon runs interference for me.'

Harry's eyes glittered. 'Simon?'

'My boss at Unbeaten Tracks. He specialises in travel to out-of-the-way places.'

'But his interest in you isn't entirely professional?'

Her friendship with Simon Fox was pleasant but casual, at least on her side. She had a feeling that Simon wanted to deepen it, but so far she wasn't sure it was what she wanted. About to confess to Harry, she felt a spark of mischief flare inside her. If Harry thought Simon cared for her maybe he would see her in a new light. It would do him good to think she hadn't been carrying a torch for him since he'd left. 'Simon and I are friends,' she said, keeping her voice carefully neutral.

His glance went to her left hand. 'But there's nothing official yet.'

A light laugh punctuated her answer. 'Maybe we do have a generation gap after all. Relationships needn't be advertised publicly any more.'

His smoke gaze carried an odd glint. 'Simon Fox is a fool if he subscribes to such drivel. If you were my woman . . .'

His voice faded and a strangling sensation took hold of Lisa's throat. 'Yes? What would you do if I were your woman?'

'I'd want my brand on you,' he said flatly. 'They say men avoid commitment, but it seems as if women are the ones who want their cake and eat it too.'

It was an effort to keep her tone light. 'Then it's just as well I'm not your woman, isn't it?' She made a show of consulting her watch. 'Good grief, I must be going. *Reef Lady* sails in an hour.'

His anger, if such it was, evaporated with her announcement. 'I'll walk you to the jetty.'

'I'd like that.' Suddenly she wanted to prolong the moment before parting. It was probably no more than an echo of her teenage crush on him, but as she stood beside him she felt so desolate that her legs almost refused to carry her through the bar to the street entrance.

'What about your luggage?' he asked when they were out in the balmy afternoon air again.

'When I flew in from Cairns this morning they told me it would be taken to *Reef Lady*. Not that I brought much for a four-day cruise, but it should be waiting in my cabin.'

'You should be well looked after on board. I told Donald Gardiner that you're a friend of mine.'

'I'm not supposed to have special treatment. My job is to report on the trip as an ordinary passenger would experience it.'

'Then I'll tell Don to reinstate the bread and water diet,' he assured her gravely.

She laughed. 'I'm glad your sense of humour is intact.'

'It gets misplaced sometimes, that's all.'

This must be one of those times, she thought ruefully. His sense of humour wasn't much in evidence this afternoon. They had spent most of it rubbing each other up the wrong way. All the same, she couldn't regret meeting him again, if only to assure herself that her teenage folly was over.

They had reached the start of the long wooden jetty which jutted out into the deeper water. Passengers were already straggling aboard the vessel moored at the far end. She turned to Harry. 'Well, this is goodbye. Or do you live in this part of the world now?'

'I live here,' he said shortly.

A memory floated to the surface. 'So you finally attained your dream,' she said, her eyes alight with pleasure. 'Your own island paradise.'

'Not entirely my own, but near enough. I share it with a few traditional owners. I'm surprised you remembered.'

'Why shouldn't I? When you told me about it you made it sound so real and attainable. I never doubted that you would make it.'

'The royalties from the book and the film rights had a lot to do with it,' he explained. 'Your father really made it possible.'

'But you wrote the book that everyone wanted to read.' On impulse she reached up and kissed him. She intended to kiss his cheek but he moved his head a fraction and her lips collided with the warmth of his mouth. The contact was fleeting but left an indelible impression on her dazed brain— like a brand, she couldn't help thinking.

She opened her eyes, hardly aware of having closed them, to find his steely gaze fixed on her face as he returned the pressure of her mouth. Just as swiftly he ended it by putting her away from him. 'Goodbye, Lisa,' he rasped. 'Have a safe journey.'

Tears glittered in her eyes as she forced herself to turn towards the jetty on leaden feet.

'Lisa, wait.'

The harsh command stayed her steps and she glanced back uncertainly. 'What is it?' Her gaze followed the line of his outstretched hand. 'Oh, no.' Tyler Thornton was showing some documents to an officer at the foot of *Reef Lady*'s gangway. The officer saluted. Shouldering a travel bag, Thornton stepped aboard.

She turned despairing eyes to Harry. 'He's going on the cruise. Now what am I going to do?'

CHAPTER TWO

'YOU could always jump ship.'

A smile hovered on Lisa's lips. 'It's tempting, but Simon expects me to report on the cruise.'

At the mention of her boss's name Harry's mouth tightened. 'The cruise runs once a week. I'm sure your friend wouldn't want you to endure a thousand miles in the company of a snake like Thornton.'

The faintly hostile emphasis he gave to the word 'friend', as applied to Simon, intrigued her. He made it sound as if this were Simon's doing when, in fact, he had urged her to take the trip to get away from Thornton for a while.

'You're right, he wouldn't,' she agreed. 'I've missed the last flight back to Cairns today but I could stay on TI overnight and fly home tomorrow.'

'If Thornton's determined to catch up with you he could be watching the airport,' he suggested.

She chewed her lower lip. 'I hadn't thought of it. You journalists are a persistent breed when you want something.'

A wintry smile lightened his features. 'I'd rather not be lumped in with Tyler Thornton, if you don't mind.'

She couldn't help smiling back. 'I don't know. You both get ten out of ten for persistence.'

His fingers curled around her upper arms and he drew her inexorably closer, so she could see the wicked gleam in his silvery gaze. 'Compared to me, Thornton doesn't know the meaning of the word persistence.'

Yet Harry hadn't been at all persistent where she was concerned. She had pursued him with single-minded purpose, only to be dismissed as a child who knew no better. Did he remember rebuffing her, or was it so unimportant to him that it wasn't etched on his consciousness, the way it was burned into hers? Rather than humiliate herself by reminding him, she angled her face away. 'I wouldn't know, would I?'

He released her and she took a stumbling step backwards, rubbing her arms as if the brief contact had bruised them. It was more likely her ego which was bruised, finding that he remembered so little of their previous encounter. To him she was a friend's daughter, a duty, nothing more. She'd forgotten how much his indifference could hurt.

Why, then, was she even considering the suggestion she knew she was about to make? 'I have some holidays owing to me. I could stay on TI for the week and join the next cruise back to Cairns. Surely Thornton will have given up by then?'

There was a moment's silence, broken by the mournful cries of the gulls wheeling overhead. Then Harry said, 'I have a better idea. Come and stay on my island for the week. There's plenty of room and you can tell your boss you're checking out a new tourist destination.'

A strange fluttering started up inside her. 'But it isn't true, is it?'

'It could be. I'm thinking of allowing a select few tourists to stay on the island, provided they appreciate the natural environment.'

Five years ago such an invitation would have made her want to turn cartwheels with joy. Now she knew better. Or did she? The idea of spending a week with Harry on his island drew her like a magnet, despite all the reasons why she shouldn't consider it. She should turn him down flat and go back to Cairns and Simon, who made no secret that he wanted her.

Vainly she tried to conjure up an image of Simon's face to counter the magnetic effect of Harry's presence. There was only a blur. With blinding clarity she knew that as long as Harry dominated her thoughts and memories there would never be room for Simon, or any other man. What better way to exorcise Harry from her life than to accept his invitation?

'Why are you doing this?' she asked, a hard edge of suspicion in her voice.

There was a far-away look in his eyes. 'I told you, I want to get Thornton off your back. Your father was part-way responsible for making the island possible and this is one way I can repay him. In his letters Nick said he hoped I'd look after you if anything happened to him. He didn't know how prophetic it would be.'

Every part of her rebelled against the idea of Harry as any sort of guardian. 'I can take care of myself. You needn't feel obligated,' she flung at him.

His shoulders rose in a suit-yourself gesture. 'There's still time to go aboard the ship.'

Her brain whirled. The vessel carried only eighty passengers. She would have little chance of avoiding Thornton aboard ship, where all meals were communal and recreation space was limited. It wasn't as if there were ports of call where she could escape him. The islands they stopped at were remote and uninhabited. She had a mental vision of Thornton pestering her all the way back to Cairns.

It wouldn't be so bad if she had anything to tell him, but she hadn't seen his mysterious photo and knew nothing about the story he wanted from her.

Harry moved purposefully on to the jetty. 'Where are you going?' she asked, jolted out of her reverie.

He glanced back over his shoulder. 'To get your luggage. Keep out of sight until I get back.'

He strode off down the wooden jetty with a confidence which left her feeling breathless. As she followed orders and retreated into the shade of a tree she was torn between anger at his arrogance and relief at having the decision taken out of her hands. Harry's island, here I come, she thought. Ready or not.

A short time later he returned with her case hefted carelessly in one hand and a broad grin on his tanned features. 'It's all set,' he announced. 'Don Gardiner will let Thornton think you're seasick the first night out. They'll be halfway to Cairns before he realises you aren't aboard.'

Four whole days free of looking over her shoulder for the tiresome journalist. It sounded wonderful. 'You think of everything,' she told Harry.

He winked at her. 'It helps to be friends with the ship's captain.'

'Which reminds me—where *did* you tell him I was staying?'

'I didn't have to. He assumed you were staying with me.'

'It sounds as if you make a habit of hijacking Captain Gardiner's passengers,' she said uneasily.

'Only the good-looking ones.'

The urge to lash out at him caught her by surprise. He was only confirming her suspicion that she was the latest of many female guests on the island. He was too well organised for one thing. And she remembered only too well his warning five years ago: 'I believe in loving and leaving before anyone gets hurt.' Anyone being him, she had assumed. Hurt by the burden of a lasting commitment.

He saw her hesitate. 'We'd better go if we're to get across Drummer Bar before sunset.'

'I don't know where your island is or how far away it is, or anything,' she said on a rising note of concern.

Amusement glittered in his smoky gaze. 'Getting cold feet, Lisa?'

'No, I . . . Should I?'

The backs of his fingers grazed her upper arm, sending shivers rippling through her. 'Probably. It isn't too late to change your mind and stay on TI.'

'Would you mind if I did?' She cursed inwardly as her voice came out infuriatingly husky.

His hooded gaze betrayed nothing. 'I can hardly object. The whole point is to keep Thornton out of your hair, so it's up to you.'

Again disappointment roiled through her. He wasn't taking her to his island to be alone with her. It was this damnable sense of obligation to her father's memory. Would he never stop treating her as the daughter of Nikita Alexandrov, and see her as she was now?

Confused, she looked away. What was going on here? She had accepted his invitation to prove to herself that she was over him. What exactly did she want from him? There was only one way to find out. 'I'll come,' she said on a sighing breath. 'But first I must make a phone call to Cairns.'

He reached for her case then straightened. 'Let me guess. You want to call Simon Fox.'

Why did he make it sound like a crime? 'His agency is paying for the cruise. I should tell him I'm not aboard so that he can change the ticket. I'll arrange to take my holidays at the same time.'

'There's a radiophone on the island. You can call him from there tomorrow.' At her surprised reaction some of his tension ebbed. 'What did you expect? Thatched huts and camp-fires?'

She pretended disappointment. 'Next you'll tell me you live in an air-conditioned condominium on the beach-front.'

He laughed and the warm velvety sound rolled over her like waves lapping the sand. 'Hardly. But Drummer Island isn't all that primitive either.'

He headed for the public moorings and she followed, taking two steps to every long stride of his. 'Was your island named after the drummer fish?' she asked.

He shook his head. 'I named it for the Thoreau quote.'

'"If a man does not keep pace with his companions, perhaps it is because he hears a different drummer. Let him step to the music he hears",' she quoted softly.

'Something of the sort.' He seemed embarrassed to have her recognise the quotation. Was it because it gave her more of an insight into Harry himself than he wanted anyone to have?

He indicated a twenty-foot cruiser riding at anchor among the dozens of boats belonging to the Thursday Islanders. Boat travel was as commonplace here as cars were elsewhere. Placing her suitcase on the deck, he helped her to negotiate the small gangway. 'Welcome aboard.'

She looked around with interest. She was standing on a covered rear deck on which was stacked fishing and scuba-diving gear. Opening off it was a compact cabin. Beyond that was a door, presumably leading to sleeping quarters. 'It's a lovely boat,' she commented.

He favoured her with a dry look. 'It's reliable and seaworthy. *You* are lovely.'

She felt herself flush. He was merely correcting her imprecise description, but the warmth in his look generated an answering heat deep inside her. This would have to stop. The whole object of the exercise was to rid herself of any lingering teenage fantasies about him, not to start creating new ones.

As they headed out to sea she watched Thursday Island until it was a speck on the horizon. Harry turned the boat north-west, towards the Arafura Sea. 'How far is it to Drummer Island?' she asked.

'About an hour from here.'

Dismay gripped her. It must be halfway to New Guinea. She'd assumed it was one of the nearby islands visible from Thursday Island.

A wave rocked them and she almost lost her balance, gripping Harry's arm as he turned the vessel bow-on to the wave. Under the tanned skin his muscles felt reassuringly solid. It was tempting to put both arms around his waist and hang on but she resisted the urge. Transferring her grip to one of the handrails, she asked, 'How many people live on the island?'

He gave her a mocking glance. 'You'll find out in an hour.'

Oh, no, surely she and Harry weren't going to be the only inhabitants of the island? Why hadn't she thought to ask before they left Thursday Island? Was it because she wanted to be alone with him?

Then she remembered his reference to the traditional owners with whom he shared the island. There must be an Aboriginal settlement of some kind there, so they wouldn't be entirely alone. She should feel relieved, but the feeling was tinged with something very like regret.

The prospect of being alone with her didn't seem to concern Harry. He seemed indifferent to her presence, making her wonder why he had suggested the trip. Her impatient sigh brought his head around. 'You'll see Drummer soon,' he misinterpreted.

She strained her eyes but could see only endless blue where the sky met the Arafura Sea. A hundred yards away the waves were sliced by a dark dorsal fin, and she shivered. Much of life on the Barrier Reef was beautiful beyond words, but it could be deadly as well.

The sight of Harry steering the vessel through the treacherous waters with relaxed confidence reassured her. Yet he was as much a newcomer here as she was. Born and bred in Melbourne, one of Australia's most populous cities, he had dreamed of living on an island in the tropics. He had been working towards his goal when they had first met.

She remembered the thrill of being taken into his confidence, seeing it as a sign of the romance about to blossom between them, when it was simply a gesture of friendship on his part. Still, she was generous enough to be glad that the royalties from her father's story had helped him to achieve his dream. Her inherited share of the rights told her how valuable they were, enabling her to have a small measure of security. No wonder Harry felt so much in her father's debt.

Her thoughts were interrupted when he gestured ahead of the boat. 'Land, ho!'

Drummer Island rose as a low crescent-shaped mound out of the Arafura Sea. The reef ran along the south-east side from a sand-spit out to the eastern tip of the jungle-clad island, sheltering a series of beaches along a semicircular bay.

Harry steered a careful course through the coral which guarded the bay mouth, then they were through into the clearest water she had ever seen. She sighted a school of manta rays winging gracefully over the surface like giant birds. As he cut the engine Harry told her they were foraging for plankton, their staple diet.

'It's paradise,' she said on a sigh. Ahead was a beach with sand as fine and white as talcum powder, fringed by giant granite boulders. The jungle reached almost to the water's edge.

Along the sand-spit, a line of casuarinas and beach hibiscus grew above the high-water mark, while native orchids clung to the rocks. Pandanus palms, paperbarks and flame trees crowded the forest. There were even a few coconut palms, although she knew these must have been imported as they weren't native to these islands.

Suddenly it didn't matter how many women Harry had brought here before her. She was here now, sharing this Eden with him, and nothing else mattered.

He anchored the cruiser a short way out from the beach and they landed in a dinghy loaded with the supplies Harry had purchased in TI that morning.

After beaching the boat expertly Harry vaulted over the side into the ankle-deep water. When she started to follow he grasped her around the waist and lifted her over the side, setting her down lightly on the sand.

She could have sworn that his hands spanned her waist longer than was absolutely necessary, and she felt again a disturbing, almost electric sense of awareness. But he turned almost immediately and began stacking the supplies above the high-water mark.

'I'll come for these once you're settled in,' he said. 'First I'll show you Casa Blake.'

'I want to see absolutely everything,' she said, unable to contain the pleasure which bubbled in her voice. Whether it was due to Harry's presence or the poetic beauty of his island, happiness overflowed inside her like a mineral spring.

'Tomorrow,' he assured her. 'Darkness falls quickly in the islands, so we won't have time tonight.'

He was right. Even as he led her along a path of crushed coral, the pearly dusk started to give way to velvet darkness. She quickened her steps.

In the grey light she glimpsed a coconut grove and fishing nets hung out to dry, then Harry led her past a shell fountain and through an arch to a palm-thatched dwelling. The dwelling blended so skilfully with its surroundings that it was barely visible until they reached it.

'Like it?'

'I feel as if I've walked on to a Tarzan film set.'

Built around a large stone fireplace, the house was spacious and airy. Blackwood posts supported a woven frond ceiling and seagrass matting softened the stone floor. The walls rose no more than waist high, with shutters which opened to the jungle beyond. Windows protected the house to seaward.

The furnishings were simple but inviting. Cane sofas and easy-chairs were arranged against a backdrop of shelves crammed with hundreds of books on every subject from philosophy to cookery. Her vision of the place as a South Pacific bachelor's delight began to crumble. Judging from the well-thumbed state of the books, Harry read himself to sleep most nights.

He sensed her astonishment. 'It isn't what you expected for a globe-trotting journalist, is it?'

She sank on to a cane chair. 'No, it isn't. But you never struck me as any sort of Robinson Crusoe.'

'Now you'll have a new opinion of me, won't you?'

Why should her opinion matter to him? It never had before. 'Don't you miss life in the fast lane?' she asked.

He gave a careless shrug. 'Everything I need is right here, especially now.'

She flashed him a curious look but he didn't elaborate. Instead he picked up her case. 'I'll show you your room so you can freshen up while I get dinner ready.'

Her room was as pleasantly tropical as the rest of the house, with cane furniture and a low bed festooned with mosquito netting. Harry deposited her case on the bed and left her to change, after pointing out the shared bathroom across the hall.

Unpacking took little time, and she regarded her clothes with dismay. They had been chosen for sunbathing on deserted islands, not for her present situation. But they would have to do. The caftan she chose for dinner was intended to cover up a bikini. It was filmy, almost transparent, so she prayed for a low level of lighting. She was prepared to reveal as much on a public beach, so what was the difference?

Harry Blake was the difference, she conceded reluctantly. Telling herself that what she felt was a hangover from a teenage crush didn't entirely convince her. Her body still reacted to his nearness in a way which brought the colour rushing to her face. She had been fighting the awareness all day and now she had to face facts. Part of her was still in love with him, no matter how much she tried to deny it.

Thrusting a brush through her heavy curtain of hair, she appraised her reflection thoughtfully. Was she really here to kick her 'Harry habit' or was she using this excuse to test deeper waters? Maybe this time... The words from the song drifted through her mind. Was she hoping that, this time, things would turn out differently?

The aroma of sizzling steak lured her out on to a stone-paved terrace where Harry was turning meat on an open-air grill.

A nearby table held salad ingredients, and she moved towards it. 'Can I help?'

'Go ahead. These will be ready in a few minutes.'

The darkness had reduced the island to an intimate circle of light which bathed them in its glow. The air vibrated with sounds, from the myriad insects homing in on the torches flickering high on bamboo poles to the sizzle of the roasting meat.

The sounds and aromas assaulted her senses which were already under siege from the sight of Harry at work. He had exchanged his moleskins for a pareu, a length of batik-printed cloth which wound around his waist like a sarong.

In the barbecue flames his upper body gleamed chestnut, every muscle as cleanly defined as a bas-relief sculpture, inviting her touch to an almost painful degree.

Flustered, she concentrated on the salad, but her fingers felt awkward as she selected ingredients. Croutons and crumbled bacon were already to hand and Harry supplied a fresh egg, so she soon had a tempting Caesar salad.

He brought a plate of steaks to the table. 'This looks good.' He scooped a crouton out of the salad and she tapped the back of his hand with a spoon. With a yelp he pressed his hand to his mouth in mock suffering. Her insides clenched in protest. It was such a waste of a good kiss.

He touched a finger to the frown etching her forehead. 'What's this? It was only a crouton.'

Her eyes brightened as she dodged his touch. '"Manners maketh the man", even on an island.'

His eyes danced. 'I can see I need you here to keep me on the straight and narrow.'

A pang shot through her. 'You don't need anyone, Harry Blake. You told me so yourself, years ago.'

The night echoed with his sigh. 'Yet you agreed to come anyway.'

'I needed *you*, remember?'

'To rescue you from Thornton.' It sounded as if he was reminding himself. He gestured impatiently. 'Are we going to talk or eat?'

Which was a neat way of changing the subject, she noticed. Picking up a plate, she added salad to the mammoth T-bone steak he'd given her, and sat down opposite him. The food occupied them for a while, then Harry cleared the plates away while she poured glasses of iced tea. It was as heady as wine in a setting where the very air was intoxicating. She inhaled appreciatively, filling her lungs with the scents of night-blooming jasmine and ornamental tobacco.

Harry tilted his chair back and cupped his hands behind his head. 'Are you happy in the travel business, Lisa?'

'Very. Having parents who'd travelled must have whetted my appetite. I loved doing the travel and tourism diploma so much that I'm now nearly through a Bachelor of business degree, majoring in tourism management.'

He whistled softly. 'The lady has brains as well as beauty.'

'That's the second time you've called me beautiful since we got here,' she commented.

'Wrong. The first time, I said you were lovely,' he corrected her. 'In this light your eyes flash with black fire.'

Driven by restlessness, she stood up. 'Why do you keep saying such things? It isn't as if you mean them. You told me yourself that women are playthings to you.'

'I said that?'

'You know you did, when you told me I was wasting my time falling in love with you.'

'Sometimes you have to be cruel to be kind.'

She whirled on him. 'It wasn't kind to throw my feelings back in my face. It took me years to regain the confidence to enjoy going out with men.'

He swore under his breath. 'It wasn't my intention.'

'While we're throwing clichés around we both know which road is paved with good intentions.' She hadn't meant to have this out with him now but it came boiling to the surface unbidden. She swallowed hard. 'It wasn't until months after you left that another cliché occurred to me. The one about always hurting the one you love.'

He seemed to sense where she was heading. 'Lisa, don't.'

She was determined to say it. 'I finally worked it out. You did care for me, didn't you? You hurt me for my benefit, not your own.'

His fingers spread wide as his body language refuted her claim. 'Lord, Lisa, if I'd known you felt this way I wouldn't have suggested bringing you here.'

'But you did suggest it, and I agreed because I must know how you really feel. Simon Fox is pressing me for a commitment and . . . damn you, you keep getting in the way.'

He heard the tears threading her voice and got to his feet. His hands were warm as they rested on her shoulders. 'I didn't know, Lisa, I swear. I wanted to help you, not start something which can't do either of us any good.'

Her anger flared. 'There you go again, telling me what's best for me when you haven't a clue what I need.'

His eyes narrowed dangerously. 'You're older and wiser now, are you?'

'I think so.'

He inched closer until she felt his breath on her cheeks. 'Is this what you want, Lisa?'

Breathing became a struggle. 'Yes, Harry. Oh, yes.'

His shadow swallowed her and his mouth devoured the rest, driving the breath from her body with its power and passion. Her bones turned liquid until only his hold kept her upright. Her mind spun. This was where she had dreamed of being for so long. Her arms tightened around his bare shoulders and her fingers dug into the warm flesh of his back. Her moan of pleasure was a soft, animal sound.

Slowly he moved her away from him, his eyes ablaze with a peculiar light. 'Would you say a kiss like that means something?'

She dragged her eyes to his face. What was he getting at? 'It did to me,' she said shakily. Then she understood the point he was making. 'Oh, God, not again.'

The mockery in his smile seared her. 'Fool me once, shame on you. Fool me twice, shame on me. That's twice, Lisa. Your judgement is way off, as I just demonstrated.'

She wished the ground would swallow her up. 'Why are you doing this?'

'To show you the dangers of reading too much into things. It's still a mistake to get entangled with me. I thought you understood.'

She scrubbed her mouth with the back of her hand. 'You're a bastard, Harry.'

'Shall I put it in writing?'

'There's no need. I doubt if I'll forget again as long as I live.' She *had* been reading too much into their situation, hoping that this time things would be different between them. She almost wished she had taken her chances with Tyler Thornton on the cruise. Whatever had made her think she would be safer with Harry Blake?

CHAPTER THREE

NIGHT on the island brought a profusion of strange sounds: the wailing of curlews on the beach, the chop-chop-chop of nightjars and the high-pitched squeals of fruit bats. The sounds made Lisa feel even more alien here.

For most of her life this fish-out-of-water feeling had tormented her. Buying her flat in Cairns had allayed it somewhat. For the first time there was somewhere she truly belonged. Now the feeling was back, thanks to Harry's rejection.

Too restless to sleep, she pushed aside the mosquito netting festooning the bed, and padded barefoot to the windows occupying half of one wall. Palms flat against the sill, she stared out at the shadow-puppet jungle, the shapes eerie against a pearlescent sky. In one night Harry had shattered illusions she hadn't acknowledged that she held. Subconsciously she *had* been waiting for his return, telling herself the only thing which had stood between them before was her youth and inexperience.

Now she faced the bitter truth. Harry was no white knight, and loving and leaving *was* his credo. She should have listened the first time. Then she would have accepted his invitation for what it was instead of letting her fantasies run away with her.

But no more. If he wanted the job of Dutch uncle it was his. No more fantasies. And no more kisses, either, she thought as her hand strayed to her mouth. It felt bruised—surely another illusion? A burning sensation rose inside her but she subdued it, telling herself he wasn't worth it. Think of Simon, she commanded her mind. No sooner had she formed an image of Simon than dark fingers of thought ripped it away and substituted a tall, spare figure with a sloping shoulder and smouldering grey eyes.

Shuddering, she pressed her palms against her eyes. 'Simon, Simon,' she chanted as if it could banish Harry's image. Repeating the times' tables would have had as much effect.

A sound at her door brought her head up. She was alone but the bamboo curtain across the opening swayed as if someone had disturbed it. There was no one there.

'Did you sleep well?' Harry asked when she joined him at breakfast next morning.

Resentment enfolded her like a stiff cloak. Unlike him, she couldn't pretend that all was well. 'Not really,' she admitted. 'The sounds of the sea and the jungle are too strange.'

'You stop noticing them after a while.'

'I also thought someone came to my bedroom door during the night.'

He cut a slice off a glistening pawpaw. 'My imagination played tricks on me when I first arrived.'

He didn't deny looking in on her, she noticed, but it must have been him. Probably his misguided sense of duty again. She decided not to challenge him about it in case he thought it mattered to her.

He set a plate of muesli in front of her and she splashed milk on to it, then toyed with it until he said, 'Eat something, for goodness' sake.'

Her look seared him. 'Yes, Uncle Harry.'

'And cut that out as well.' He slammed a knife on to the table with such force that she jumped. 'I don't want you getting the wrong idea about me, but you needn't go to the other extreme, either.'

'Make up your mind,' she murmured under her breath.

Whether he heard or not, his expression softened and his hand slid under her chin, forcing her to look at him. 'I suppose it's too much to expect for us to be friends?'

Gritting her teeth against the tears blurring her vision, she nodded then found her voice with an effort. 'Is it what Papa wanted?'

'No, damn it, it's what I want.'

What Harry wanted he usually got. Well, not this time. She stood up. 'I won't be needing the radio-phone after all. I've decided to go back to TI today.'

He massaged the beard shadowing his chin. 'I guess you've answered my question.'

'Then you'll take me back?'

'Not possible, I'm afraid. There's the weather to contend with.'

Her glance flew to the impossibly blue sky feathered with high white clouds. 'The weather's perfect.'

His face muscles twitched but he nodded gravely. 'Agreed. But if you walk out along the sand-spit you'll see a great curling sea running, a swell,' he elaborated. 'With any sort of sea running it's dangerous trying to cross Drummer Bar. If it happens when I've gone to the mainland I'm cut off from the island until the swell dies down.'

She sat down abruptly. 'Then I'm stuck here. For how long?'

'Until it's safe to cross.' He gave a wintry smile. 'You look as if you don't believe me.'

'It is extremely convenient, especially since I'm not enough of a sailor to argue with you.'

With a long-suffering sigh he grasped her hand and urged her to her feet. 'Come with me.'

Since her hand was trapped in his vice-like grip, she had little option. He led her to an alcove off the main room. On a desk was a metal unit equipped with switches and dials and what appeared to be a telephone handset. Releasing her, Harry worked the switches until a crackling voice flooded the room. It was a local news broadcast and ended with a warning to shipping. Harry flicked it off. 'Satisfied?'

'Yes, thank you. What do we do now?'

'We wait it out, if possible without biting each other's head off in the process.'

She resisted the urge to apologise. 'I can manage it if you can,' she said pointedly.

He held out his hand. 'It's a deal.'

As briefly as possible she touched her fingers to his, trying to ignore the electrical sensation which pulsed along her arm. The sensation compounded her dismay. She had counted on returning to TI today while she could still salvage some pride. She hadn't bargained on being trapped here.

'Could you show me how to use the radio-phone?' she asked. 'I really should call Simon.'

His dark eyes glittered then were hooded. Without comment he showed her which switches allowed her to speak and listen. Then he moved towards the terrace. 'Call me if you need anything.'

Some demon made her say, 'There's no need to leave. It isn't a private call.'

All the same he left her alone, although she wondered if he could overhear the conversation anyway. Then she chided herself. She was assuming that he cared what she said to Simon Fox. It would only matter if he were interested in her himself, and they both knew he wasn't. Simon's voice came on the line, forcing her attention back to the radiophone. 'Where did you say you were?'

'Drummer Island,' she repeated through the static. 'Tyler Thornton joined the cruise at TI so I decided to wait and take the next one back to Cairns.'

'Good idea,' Simon echoed. 'I don't know this Drummer place. It must be new.'

'It's not open to the public yet,' she explained. 'I'm checking it out as a possible destination.'

'Good idea.' Simon sounded pleased. 'Who owns it?'

She glanced towards the terrace but Harry was out of sight. 'No one you know,' she said on a heavy sigh. 'But the owner is amenable to selective visits. I'll tell you all about it when I get back.'

'Take as long as you like. It's time you had a holiday,' Simon volunteered, then his voice dropped. 'I'll miss you, though.'

A shadow moved on the terrace. 'I know, I'll miss you, too.' She could almost feel Simon's startled reaction down the line. His feelings for her were an open secret but it was the first time she'd given him the slightest encouragement. She wished there were an answering flicker inside her but she felt empty instead. She couldn't go on. 'I'll see you soon,' she promised.

'If Thornton shows up at the agency I'll tell him you're away. He must head south sooner or later.'

'You're an angel, Simon.' This time sincerity came easily. 'His paper must be sick of funding his jaunt around the reef with no results.'

'Take care of yourself, darling. Don't work too hard on this new destination. Take some time off as well.'

'I will.' There was a long pause during which she sensed he was waiting for some kind of endearment from her. The words stalled in her throat. 'Goodbye, Simon.'

When she signed off her throat was tight with tears. She wished she hadn't encouraged Simon. No matter how kind and nice he was, he wasn't for her.

It would serve her right if he didn't want to employ her any more after she told him so. And all because she had wanted to give Harry something to overhear.

He was cleaning some diving equipment when she rejoined him. He didn't seem troubled by what he'd heard. 'How did it go?'

'Fine. I didn't expect any problems.'

He looked up from polishing the face-plate of a diving mask. 'Did he offer to join you here?'

Her eyebrows arched. 'No. Why should he?'

'It's what I would have done if you were my woman.'

Did he suspect that her conversation with Simon was mainly for his benefit? 'Simon trusts me,' she said.

There was irony in the gaze he directed at her. 'Of course, but what about me?'

'You made your position crystal-clear last night,' she snapped, annoyed with herself for the betraying emotion which charged her voice.

Cynicism coloured his expression. 'Fox doesn't know that, does he?'

As he walked away she shot a lethal look at his back, taunted by the bronzed, muscular expanse. His point was clear. If Simon loved her he wouldn't trust her to strangers on a lonely island. The thought had occurred to her, too, but there was no need for Harry to rub it in. Just because he didn't love her didn't mean no man ever would.

The day stretched ahead endlessly. She decided to do what she came here for—assess the island's potential as a tourist destination. She emerged from her room, notebook in hand and straw hat dangling around her neck, when Harry appeared. 'I hope it's all right for me to take a look around.'

'I'll join you.'

The last thing she wanted was his company when her mind was in such turmoil. 'There's no need. I can find my own way,' she demurred.

Hostility flashed in his eyes. 'It *is* my island. I'd like to show you around.'

There might be parts of it he wanted kept private. She decided to accept his company but keep things as coolly professional as possible between them. 'I'd appreciate a guided tour, if I'm not taking up too much of your time.'

He gave vent to a long-suffering sigh. 'I invited you here, remember? When you're imposing I'll let you know.'

She didn't doubt it, since he had already warned her against trespassing on his love-life. She had never met anyone with as many 'keep out' signs around them as Harry. They might be invisible but they were there all the same.

Well, she could put up a few of her own. 'I'm ready; lead the way,' she said in a tone devoid of warmth.

His garden was terraced on a ridge behind the house. Tracks branched off in several directions, the widest one leading down to the beach. He indicated a path leading to a high look-out rock. 'I'll show you the spring first.'

He led the way up a gently graded pathway made of crushed shells, and out over a granite headland which offered a spectacular view. 'There should be a seat here so that you could sit and soak this up,' she said, her voice cracking.

'There will be soon. I'm carting sandstone blocks up to make a bench right there.'

Several blocks were already in place, she noticed now. She imagined sitting here in quiet meditation, watching the Arafura Sea in all its moods. She shook herself free of the spell. Once she reported back to Simon she would probably never return. 'You mentioned a spring,' she said briskly.

The main water supply was located in a small, steep gully about thirty metres above sea level. Here Harry had built a small tank as a catchment for rainwater. Plastic piping led from the tank down the hill towards the house. Her eyebrows lifted. 'Is this your handiwork?'

He nodded. 'This spring is the only reliable source of fresh water on this side of the island. There are others but they tend to vanish during the dry season. This gives me enough water to last through the summer.'

She remembered her mission. 'Is there enough for visitors as well?'

'Sure, provided everyone is careful. You couldn't shower six times a day, but there's enough for most normal needs.'

'Is it good to drink?'

'Try it and see.' He produced a wooden goblet and dipped it into the tank. Droplets glistened on the cup as he handed it to her. Thirsty from the climb, she drank eagerly. 'It's wonderful. You could bottle and sell it,' she enthused.

He took the cup from her. 'Sometimes pure rainwater beats the finest champagne.' Dipping the cup again, he drank from it. Her mouth dried as she watched. Sharing the cup was like being kissed by him. She could feel the warmth of his mouth on her lips, and her tongue darted out to moisten them.

He swallowed the last of the water and she swallowed too, her throat closing at the sight of his fingers tight around the cup, while moisture gleamed on his upper lip like a crystal moustache.

He wiped his mouth with the back of his hand, breaking the spell. 'Drummer Island is almost self-sufficient. Would you like to see the rest?'

Unable to summon her voice, she nodded, and he regarded her curiously. Then he plunged on past the spring to a patch of swampy ground. 'I grow taro here, a root vegetable not unlike potato. My hens supply eggs, and there's a stand of bananas, breadfruit, pawpaws, oranges and limes, as well as fresh vegetables in season.'

The plantation was an extension of the jungle, and she had glimpsed it on the way to the spring. 'It's perfect,' she murmured. 'I'm surprised you can think of sharing it with outsiders.'

'I'm not rich. It will help if the island can pay its way,' he explained. 'It also seems selfish for one person to have all this when it can give pleasure to many. I thought of taking six guests at a time. What do you think?'

'Six is just right. They can practically have a beach to themselves. Think of it—no newspapers, radio or television, just the beauty of nature on your doorstep.' Her thoughts raced furiously. 'I can think of quite a few people who'll appreciate coming here. Overseas visitors are always asking us for novel destinations. It's the reason why Simon started up Unbeaten Tracks.'

Harry's sharp gaze pierced her. 'This is nothing to do with Simon Fox. I want you to arrange everything; only you.'

Her palms spread in an agitated gesture. 'This puts me in an awkward spot. Simon's my boss. I'm here as his representative.'

'No, you aren't. You're here as my guest. Didn't he tell you to take some time off?'

Why was he making things difficult for her? 'Yes, he did, but——'

'You're taking it,' he interrupted as if the question were settled. 'If I choose to give you exclusive rights to the island it's my business. You don't want to work for someone else all your life, do you?'

She rested her back against a sun-warmed sandstone cliff. 'No, I'd like to have my own agency one day.'

'Then you have to start somewhere.' His eyes were hooded but she could feel his scrutiny from under the lowered lids. 'Unless, of course, you're afraid to strike out on your own.'

A sense of *déjà vu* swept over her. At nineteen she'd contemplated a career as a teacher until he'd

accused her of being afraid to try her wings outside
the education system. Spurred on by his challenge,
she had become a travel agent. Was history about
to repeat itself? 'I'm not afraid,' she said with quiet
determination. 'I'm waiting for the right time.'

With his bladed hand he made a chopping
motion. 'The time is never right. First you do, then
you find out whether you can or not. Have you
ever regretted not becoming a teacher?'

'No,' she conceded. 'I love travel, seeing new
places and helping people to enjoy themselves. And
I do teach, at the local technical college.'

'Which proves my point—no pain, no gain.' He
shifted impatiently. 'Did you get to Russia to meet
your relatives?'

'It's still on my list. Now that *glasnost* has sim-
plified things I might be able to go back and meet
some of my relatives.' Her tone grew wistful.
'Mama always wanted me to. Did you know that
she used to work in the Kremlin in Moscow?'

'She was a civil service secretary in the Export
Trade Secretariat before she met your father,' Harry
confirmed.

Mist filmed her eyes. 'Of course, you went into
all that for your book. I'd love to see the Kremlin.
All those wonderful centuries-old cathedrals with
their golden cupolas and palace windows shining
like mirrors. Imagine climbing Ivan's Belfry and
finding all of Moscow at your feet. Sorry, I'm
getting carried away.'

His smile indulged her. 'I've been to Moscow
myself. It's enough to carry anyone away.'

'Mama wanted me to see it. Maybe she and Papa courted there.'

He looked thoughtful. 'They did most of their courting on a cruise to Khimki, one of the few places where you can get sleeping accommodation without an ID. It's very popular with romantic young couples.'

Colour seeped into her cheeks. It was hard to think of her parents as romantic youngsters. Maybe all children felt the same. They were simply Mama and Papa.

He gave her a sharp-eyed glance. 'Do you still regret not knowing your relatives?'

She had confessed as much when she'd helped him to research her father's life-story. 'I know I'm wishing for the moon, but I still wonder about them. Especially on the important holidays when other families gather together. But at least I had my parents. They had no one. I know Mama missed her sister, Lyudmila, the most. They grew up in Zagorsk and their papa took them to Gorky Park to ride the Ferris wheel and eat blinis. Whenever Mama made blinis with carrot jam she got hugely nostalgic.'

'While you just got huge on her cooking,' Harry said with a laugh.

His friendly tone defused any resentment on her part. Besides, he was right. She had gorged herself on her mother's rich Russian cooking until she'd understood the reasons behind it. 'Not any more,' she said firmly. 'It's *nouvelle cuisine* for me these days.'

His eyes swept over her curves, outlined by her T-shirt and fashionable shorts. 'The results are worth it.'

His obvious appreciation sent waves of heat surging through her, but she drove them back. Coolly professional, she reminded herself. A discussion of her figure hardly qualified.

'What else should I see here?' she asked, managing to keep the huskiness out of her voice by sheer will-power.

The slightest hesitation preceded his answer. 'Would you like to see the real Drummer Island?'

Her gaze went from the taro swamp behind them to the limitless vistas of ocean and sand at their feet. 'There's more?'

'You haven't seen the best part yet. It's under the sea.'

Fear shafted through her. 'You mean go diving on the reef?'

'Snorkelling. It's quite safe and an experience you'll never forget, I promise you.'

If she lived through it, she thought, recalling the ominous dorsal fin she'd seen slicing through the water. 'What about the surf you were worried about?'

'Swell,' he corrected her. 'It doesn't affect the lagoon, and there are no sharks inside the bar,' he added, as if sensing the reason for her reluctance.

'Are you sure?'

'Positive. Will you trust me to teach you?'

He asked a lot from someone who suffered from terminal insecurity. Not only had she never dived before, but it took a lot to get her to the top floor of a high-rise building. Another consequence of her insecure childhood, she assumed.

If anyone else had suggested it she would have turned them down flat, but Harry was doing the asking. Standing before her, he was the image of solid dependability. The certainty had no logical basis, but she knew he would never allow her to come to harm. 'I'll do it,' she said in a rush.

Although she rarely ventured outside freshwater pools, she was a strong swimmer. Her aerobics classes would help, too, Harry explained, as they improved her lung capacity.

She paid close attention while he fitted her with flippers which made her graceless on land but which he assured her would propel her effortlessly through the water. After wetting them for easier fitting he made her sit on a rock and dangle her feet in the water, moving them backwards and forwards until the flippers felt comfortable and secure.

Remembering to breathe through her mouth was trickier, but she was reminded the first time the glass face-plate misted over. Harry cleared it for her then refitted it, adding a J-shaped snorkel tube which he clipped to the side of her mask. Through it she could see clearly with her face in the water, while breathing through the tube which protruded above the waves.

Only once did the tube fill with water, choking her, but Harry showed her how to keep it clear by using her tongue to block the tube. Then he made her straighten and blow the water out before she resumed breathing as before.

'Now you're ready for the big time,' he said.

She contemplated the vast ocean breaking roughly over the coral bar at the entrance of the lagoon. 'Not out there?'

'I thought you'd agreed to trust me?'

Her breath escaped in a rush. 'I do. I'm ready.'

'Good girl.' Carrying her gear, she followed him along the waterswept raft of sand and coral until he stopped at a place where the sea foamed against the rocks. Beyond it was a lagoon of almost calm water. 'The Aborigines call this the Dreaming Pool,' he told her.

She saw why as soon as they donned masks and flippers and entered the pool. Lit from above, the scene had the innocence of a Botticelli painting. She almost expected to see angels dancing on the surface. Instead tiny fish painted in bright enamel colours swung to and fro in the current like baubles on a coral Christmas tree.

Harry threaded a piece of meat on to a short spear and approached the mouth of a coral cave. Her eyes widened as a moray eel emerged from its lair. She would have beaten a hasty retreat but for Harry's insistent gesture to stay.

The eel, its body as thick as a man's thigh, arched its neck and snapped at the food on the end of Harry's spear. The powerful canine jaws tore at the meat, then the eel withdrew into its lair and gulped. She could see the food moving down its throat. Moments later it slithered out for another offering.

When the eel was bloated with food it began to store the titbits in its hole for later. Finally all the meat was gone and Harry signalled for them to surface.

Gulping the salt-laden air, she pushed her mask back on to her hair. 'I've never seen anything so amazing,' she gasped. 'Are all moray eels that friendly?'

He tossed his spear and snorkel on to a rock. 'Not all. Some are quite savage, but I've befriended this one. I named her Sweetheart.'

Lisa laughed. 'Assuming she *is* female, isn't it overly intimate for an eel?'

Humour danced in his eyes. 'You know what they say? That's a moray.'

Linking her thumbs, she palmed a wave of sea water at him, catching him full in the face. 'I'll give you a moray.'

'Oh, you will, will you?'

She should have known better than to challenge him in his own domain. Before she could swim more than a few strokes away he dived and came up underneath her. Her kicks and protestations were to no avail. She was clamped against his chest, her arms pinned to her sides.

His chest was slick with water and his swimming trunks clung to him, defining his masculine form with breathtaking obviousness. Breathing was an effort suddenly. She felt limp and boneless in his hold, her flippers trailing in the water as if she were a mermaid he'd captured in the pool. She had a sense of living a fantasy as he carried her to shore.

Setting her down on the sun-toasted sand, he stripped her of flippers and mask, then bent over her, his eyes glittering fiercely. Desire ripped through her, catching her unawares. She was sure he could read her response in her face. What had happened to cool professionalism?

He was no more composed than she was. His breathing was fast and shallow, and muscles in his jaw worked as if he was fighting a battle with himself. Whatever it was, she recognised the instant when he stopped fighting. His mouth loomed closer and her world turned incandescent. The tip of her tongue darted along her lips and she heard his indrawn gasp of response.

'This wasn't what I planned,' he ground out.

She hadn't planned it either and she would probably live to regret it, but she no more wanted him to stop than the eel had wanted him to withdraw the food supply. 'Is this a moray?' she asked in a strangled voice.

It was as if she'd flung down a challenge. Sparks of light flared in his eyes as he pulled her against the hard wall of his chest. 'No, it isn't. This is *amore*.'

CHAPTER FOUR

RESPONDING to the pressure of Harry's hand against the small of her back, Lisa arched reflexively against him. Sea water beaded his face and there was a line of salt on his upper lip. She traced it with a finger and he drew a sharp breath.

His teeth closed around her finger and he pulled the tip of it deeper, sending a shudder convulsing through her. Her free hand slid around his neck so that she could urge his face down to her.

Her breasts were crushed against his chest, which was slick with salt water. The effect was mildly abrasive, sending eddies of sensation racing through her. When he kissed her the salt taste stayed on her lips until she licked it off.

He gave a groan of capitulation and slid a hand under the cup of her bikini top, starting a massaging motion which threatened to drive her out of her mind. Just when she reached the brink of mindless pleasure his touch turned teasing, coaxing her down from the heights, only to drive her even higher with his next knowing caress.

The scents of sea, sand and shore filled her nostrils and she inhaled deeply, wanting to remember every detail for the rest of her life. Harry might deny that he wanted her, but the truth burned in his gaze and throbbed through his heated touch.

They belonged together. She knew it as surely as she knew her own name. Nothing he could say could alter the fact.

His fingers raked through the damp strands of her hair, smoothing them away from her face. Then he rained kisses on her upturned nose before ravaging her mouth as if he could never taste enough of her. 'Lisa, my Lisa.' His voice was thrillingly husky.

'Love me, Harry.' It was a cry from her heart.

He lifted his head, his expression troubled. 'Are you sure you know what you're asking?'

'I'm asking you to love me.' If he didn't respond soon she would be imploring him, her pride in shreds.

'I can't offer you forever. There's no happy ever after.' His warning was tempered by the contradictory thrust of his hard body against her thigh. She could almost feel the tug of war taking place inside him.

'I can't deny I'd like a happy ever after,' she admitted, cupping her palm to his jawline. She felt his shudder under her hand. 'But I'll take whatever you want to give me, Harry.'

Amusement lightened his steely gaze. 'You're only saying that to get your own way.'

Yes, she was. Excitement gripped her as his iron control wavered. This time it *would* be different. This time he would grant her her heart's desire, and she would know what it meant to be loved by him. She felt the sweet stirrings of her own power. 'A

woman's entitled to her own way some of the time,'
she teased.

His kisses trailed across her forehead. 'Who
taught you such nonsense?'

'You did.'

He lifted his head, his eyes bright with surprise.
'How? When?'

'When you convinced me to set goals and follow
them, not letting anything stand in my way.'

His growl of dismay resonated through her. 'I
didn't have myself in mind as your target.'

She nuzzled his ear playfully. 'You make it sound
as if it's all my fault.'

'It is. If you weren't so wickedly beautiful and
desirable it would be easy to leave you alone.'

His weight pressed down on her, making her
vividly aware of his need for her. 'I like the way
you leave me alone,' she murmured, dropping her
head back in ecstasy as his mouth grazed the sensitive cleft between her breasts.

'I should,' he said half to himself. 'But you're a
fever in my blood. You drive me crazy, Lisa.'

Not half as crazy as he drove her, she thought
wildly as his fingers worked the strings of her bikini
top loose. They fell away and he skimmed a finger
around her unfettered breasts, sending her senses
amok. 'I'm not a child any more,' she said on a
taut breath of desire. 'My father trusted you, and
I do, too. I know you'll always do what's right for
us both.'

Her words had a galvanic effect on him. 'What's
right for us is not what we're doing now,' he as-

serted, jack-knifing into a sitting position. When she tried to touch him she met iron resistance.

Disappointment lanced through her. Didn't he realise the depths of her torment? 'You're wrong,' she said, bitterness sharpening her tone. 'You're not my guardian, no matter what my father asked of you. If you were I couldn't feel the way I do about you. I know you wouldn't do anything to hurt me.'

'Which is precisely why I'm asking you to go back to the house.'

Her confused gaze searched his face, but his expression was impassive. 'You really want me to go?'

'Yes, now.' To stab his point home he swivelled and clasped his arms around his bent knees, staring out to sea with blinkered determination.

What had she done to deserve his rejection? This time he couldn't use her youth as an excuse. She had aroused him, she knew it. And she had offered herself to him with an abandon which made her face flame when she thought about it. No strings, so he couldn't accuse her of wanting more from him than he wanted to give.

Therefore the flaw must be in herself. With a strangled cry she snatched up her bikini top, tied it in place and fled back towards the house. Although she willed herself not to look back, she sensed that he was still sitting on the rocky foreshore, staring out to sea. His loneliness crashed in on her like a tidal wave. She could *feel* it all the way back to the house. Yet he had walled himself off from her. However lonely he might be, it seemed he preferred it to letting her in.

Nothing moved in the rain forest as she made her way along the crushed-shell path. The air had a leaden quality, in contrast to the glorious freshness of the morning. The heavy sea over Drummer Bar must have warned of a storm on the way.

The heavy stillness seemed appropriate, reflecting her thunderous mood. How many times was she going to throw herself at Harry and suffer his rejection before she accepted that he didn't want her?

Head down, she stormed through the main room towards the bathroom, then froze as a skittering sound came from the kitchen area. Hairs lifted on the back of her neck. Harry couldn't have beaten her back to the house, so who was making the noise?

When she saw the culprit a smile broke through her wintry expression. A pitta bird was foraging for crumbs along the counter top. Usually shy, the birds dwelt on the forest floor. She had heard their cheery 'hello and wake up' whistle in the early morning. She almost laughed aloud as the bird preened itself in front of Harry's shaving mirror. And well it might. The combination of chestnut brown, black head, green back, blue shoulders and scarlet underside was dazzling.

Hearing her, the bird gave a startled whistle and flew away over the waist-high wall. She wanted to call after it to come back, she was a friend.

The connection was instantaneous. Harry was acting just like the bird, retreating as a reflex action. It occurred to her that there could be more to his rejection than she knew. He could have been badly hurt in the past. But, even if it was true, what could she do about it?

She resolved not to think about it until she'd had a shower and washed off the salt water drying on her skin, making it feel tight and gritty. She made the shower a quick one. Although tempted to linger under the tepid spray, she remembered Harry's injunction about conserving water.

The cleansing spray, brief though it was, washed away some of her frustration. Her thinking was clearer by the time she emerged, swathed in a bath towel with another towel turbaning her hair. Beneath the towel her legs were a satisfying shade of brown from careful doses of the tropical sun. The island life agreed with her, outwardly at least. Inwardly she wasn't so sure. Until she knew why Harry was so determined to keep her at arm's length she would have no inner peace.

There was no sign of him as she padded barefoot through the house, leaving a faint trail of damp footprints across the matting. At his bedroom door she paused. Maybe his room could tell her something that Harry couldn't.

His room was the twin of hers, with a woven-frond ceiling supported by blackwood posts, seagrass matting underfoot, and waist-high stone walls with shutters left open to the jungle beyond. A glossy black native starling gave her a flame-eyed look of distrust before abandoning the wall for the safety of the trees.

She moved deeper into the room. The furniture was spartan. A low double bed of bleached pine was covered, incongruously, she thought, by a rainbow-coloured Ken Done quilt. What had she expected—satin sheets?

There was a desk and pine chest topped by a framed mirror, a straight-backed pine chair and an alcove screened by sliding louvre doors which served as a built-in wardrobe. The contents were arranged with almost military precision while an overnight bag sat open, packed and ready for use at short notice, on the floor. Once a journalist, always a journalist, she thought wryly.

The chest of drawers held more promise. On top was a collection of typically male paraphernalia: keys, a wallet, black plastic comb, a matchbook from a Cairns restaurant, and a palm-sized leather notebook, the tooling on the front worn almost smooth.

With a sense of foreboding she reached for the notebook and flipped it open. In the space for an owner's address the details had been crossed out and rewritten until they were nearly illegible. The crowded pages bulged with reminder slips.

In a scratched plastic sleeve at the back were several photos which she eased out. One showed a small boy in Scout's uniform between two adults. Harry and his parents? The look of grim determination was unmistakable even at such a young age. It was Harry, all right.

The second photo drove the breath from her body as if she had been punched. It was a wedding photo and the groom was Harry Blake. He looked devastatingly attractive in a grey dress suit as he gazed lovingly at a raven-haired woman in a white gown. Beneath her veil her eyes shone with a joy which sent spears of jealous recognition shafting through Lisa.

How often had she surprised that same look in her own reflection whenever she thought of Harry? The woman loved Harry and he loved her enough to marry her. A roaring in her ears drowned out the birdsong. Helpless rage flooded through her as her fingers spasmed around the photograph. It took all of her will-power not to crush it into nonexistence.

'Looking for something?'

She spun around, her eyes glazed with shock. Harry swam into focus in the doorway. He was blazingly angry. Two strides brought him to her. She gasped as he ripped the photo from her hand. 'What the hell do you think you're doing?'

'Trying to understand.' The admission was forced from her aching throat as tears threatened to spill over. 'I need to know why you don't want me.' There, it was said. She averted her eyes to hide the humiliation flaring in them.

'What makes you think I don't want you?' His voice softened, drawing her head up in astonishment.

He had pulled a pair of canvas shorts over his swimming trunks and they moulded his tanned hips.

His chest was bare. It was all she could do not to run her fingers across it. 'I wanted you to make love to me.'

'Just because I didn't it doesn't mean I don't want to.'

The room lurched crazily. 'Is it because of your wife?' Saying the words gave them a reality which rocked her to her core. She wanted to curl up on his bed, wrap her arms around her legs, and cry herself into oblivion.

Granite would have possessed more vitality than his expression as he nodded once. 'Yes.'

'You must love her very much.'

Again, a single taut nod. 'As much as it's possible for a man to love a woman.'

She had come in search of truth but had never expected it to hurt as much as this. 'I see. She was standing in our way, wasn't she?' It had never occurred to Lisa that he was comparing her to another woman, and found her wanting.

He thrust the photo into a drawer and slammed it shut as if closing the door on a painful memory. 'Kim will always stand in the way,' he said harshly.

Perhaps she wouldn't release him from their marriage. Perhaps, and the thought wrenched at her, perhaps there were children to consider. 'But I didn't ask you for marriage, only that you love me.' Was even that asking for the moon? 'Lots of people live together without commitment nowadays.' Try as she might, she couldn't keep the bitterness out of her voice. She had told herself she would settle for whatever he was offering, but it sounded such a poor bargain when spoken aloud.

A hard laugh punctuated his answer. 'You're such a woman of the world these days, Lisa. Did Simon Fox convince you that love without marriage is a modern ideal?'

'Simon wants to marry me,' she said stiffly.

'Then why don't you accept?'

'Because I don't love Simon.' As soon as the words were out she knew they were true. 'I love——'

A hand clamped tightly over her mouth, stifling the sound. 'Don't say it. I don't want to hear it.'

The salt tang of his palm stayed on her lips after she shook herself free. 'A truth remains true even when it's unspoken.' He must know by now that he couldn't stop her from loving him just because he willed it? She'd had five years to prove him wrong. 'Are you still married, Harry?'

A snarl twisted his mouth. 'Haven't you worked it out yet? Kim's dead.'

The admission was wrung from him with such force that she reeled back as if from a blow. 'How long?' she managed to whisper.

'Seven years ago, just before I met your father,' he ground out. His eyes glittered with a ferocity which made her quail. How powerfully he must have loved his wife to grieve for her for so long.

It almost killed her to ask, but she had to know. 'What happened?'

'You may not like the answer.'

'Not knowing is worse.'

He inclined his head then swung his dark gaze back to her. 'You may not think so once you know the truth. Kim is dead because I killed her.'

'Harry, no!'

Her tortured response was made to an empty room. On the heels of his admission he spun away, over the low stone wall into the jungle beyond. She heard his crashing passage through the undergrowth.

She stayed frozen where she was for almost a full minute, until a breeze on her damp skin sent shivers sweeping through her. She cursed her scanty covering which stopped her from pursuing him. He had no right to make such a confession then leave her to deal with it alone. There must be more. She refused to believe that Harry Blake had killed anyone.

Her fingers trembled as she pulled on shorts and a T-shirt. They refused to deal with a bra so she left it off, desperate to go in search of Harry.

She found him on the pathway leading to the spring. He was hunkered down on the cliff-top, where she had suggested building a look-out. His far-sighted stare seemed oblivious to the magnificent view. His skin was sallow under his tan. He didn't acknowledge her presence when she dropped down beside him.

'You have to tell me the rest,' she pleaded.

His bleak stare raked her. 'I don't have to do anything.'

A sigh escaped her parted lips. She was the one who wanted to know it all. Had her insistence destroyed any chance of an understanding between them? 'You're right, you don't,' she conceded. 'But I hope you'll want to tell me the rest. It may help to talk about it.'

'Talking can't restore a life.'

'But it can restore some semblance of tranquillity.' At that moment she wasn't sure whether she meant his state of mind or her own. 'I can't believe you killed anyone, Harry,' she said with quiet insistence.

'Still as sweetly naïve as ever, aren't you?' he drawled, his voice dripping sarcasm.

Something snapped inside her and she scrambled to her feet. With legs wide apart and hands planted on hips she glared down at him. 'I'm neither sweet nor naïve, simply objective. The Harry Blake I know wouldn't consciously hurt anyone.'

He massaged his chin thoughtfully. 'Ah, but there's the rub.'

Her arms dropped to her sides. 'What are you saying?'

His hand encircled her wrist and he pulled her back down beside him. 'I'm saying you hit the nail on the head when you said I wouldn't consciously hurt anyone. But I might as well have done. Kim died because of me, so it's the same thing.'

She was glad to be sitting down as a wave of weakness swept over her. She had known that Harry wasn't capable of murder, but for some reason he blamed himself for his wife's death. 'How did it happen?' she asked.

'I was working on a story about organised crime, going undercover as a courier to get the information I needed. The stuff was explosive—names, case histories, enough evidence for the police to make some arrests.'

'I think I remember the series. You got as many headlines as your stories did.' She remembered the shock of seeing him interviewed on a current-affairs programme. Even then his personal power mesmerised her, although she couldn't imagine the impact he would have on her own life.

'The publicity was the problem,' he said, his voice cracking at the memories which were obviously still painful. 'I started getting phone calls telling me to drop the series or my family would suffer.'

Her heart felt heavy as she sensed what was coming. 'You didn't stop, did you?'

He clenched his fists so tightly that the knuckles whitened. 'I *knew* these people and what they were capable of, but I told myself the public good was more important.'

She covered his clenched fist with her own, and massaged it gently, persuasively. 'You put criminals behind bars, where they couldn't hurt any more people.'

'Except Kim,' he said with savage intensity. 'I gambled with her life and I lost. Her car exploded one morning as she was setting off for work. The destruction was so total that the police couldn't establish a cause, far less identify the perpetrator. But they were certain her car was booby-trapped.'

It came back to Lisa now. 'I remember reading about it, but the woman referred to wasn't Kim Blake.'

'She was a journalist in her own right and worked under her maiden name after we married. As a reporter herself she insisted we couldn't give in to extortion. She paid the price for my principles.'

'They were her principles, too. She could have asked you to drop the whole thing, but she didn't because she believed in what you were doing. It was her choice.'

'But the decision should have been mine. The scum I was after knew I wouldn't be stopped by threats to my own life, so they targeted someone close to me.'

Without thinking, she dropped her hands to his shoulders and began to knead the knotted muscles under the tanned skin. His tension radiated along her fingers and up her forearms as a dull ache which she welcomed as a way of sharing his burden. Her palms slid along the tops of his shoulders, her thumbs and fingers finding the pressure points which would temper his suffering. 'Is what happened to Kim the reason why you gave up investigative journalism?'

He flexed his shoulders, leaning in to her touch as if it was a welcome relief. 'Mostly. The series on the immigrants was the last under my byline.'

'No wonder you welcomed the chance to write Papa's story,' she mused. 'I used to wonder why a hot-shot reporter like Harry Blake chose to write the biography of a Russian defector.'

Over his shoulder his hooded gaze flicked to her then back to the ocean. 'I wanted to write your father's story. It wasn't a second-best option, nor was it a form of running away.'

Her palms glowed with the heat from his body, and breathing had become difficult suddenly. 'I never thought it was.' He sounded as if he needed to convince himself as much as her.

'I just don't want anyone else to get hurt on my account,' he affirmed.

'At least now I understand.'

He shrugged her hands away, moving to his feet with a fluid motion. 'What do you understand?'

She ignored the sarcasm lacing his tone. 'I understand why you don't want to make promises to me, not now and not before. My age was never an issue, was it?'

'You were a kid, too young and innocent to get involved with a hard-bitten newspaperman like me.'

'You were never hard-bitten. But Kim's death was still fresh when we first met. No wonder you didn't want to get involved with anyone who could be used as a weapon against you.'

He mimicked silent applause. 'Give the lady a psychology degree. No, I didn't—and don't—want to get involved with anyone again.'

His words held an awful finality which sent a chill sliding down her spine. 'Why did you invite me here if you didn't want to get involved?' she demanded.

He jammed his hands into the pockets of his shorts and fixed his steely gaze on the ocean. 'I thought you'd outgrown your feelings for me. I wanted to get you out of Tyler Thornton's sights,

but there were probably a dozen better ways I could
have done it.'

Outrage swept through her as she leapt to her
feet, her Tartar blood singing in her ears. 'That's
garbage and you know it. You didn't bring me here
out of a sense of duty. It was an excuse to test
yourself in the face of temptation. Well, you've
proved your point, so you can send me back now
with a clear conscience. I'm glad to have been of
service.'

She whirled away, tears stinging her eyes, but was
brought up short by a hand clamped around her
arm. When he swivelled her to face him a storm
blazed in his dark eyes. 'You don't know what
you're talking about.'

She quailed in the face of his fury but lifted her
chin determinedly. 'Can't you see that the work
you're doing now makes your enforced sainthood
totally unnecessary?'

'How do you know what work I'm doing now?'

'When I went into your room I saw a manuscript
on your dresser. It's a book, isn't it?'

'As it happens, yes.'

'A book about the world's best-kept secrets,' she
pressed on, recalling the title page. 'Hardly a
subject to interest the criminal element.'

'Nor is it a book on stamp collecting,' he threw
at her. 'Some people might prefer to keep their
secrets.'

Her hands lifted in helpless despair. 'Must you
always write about controversial subjects?'

He gave a lop-sided shrug. 'I write what needs to be written. The best books usually get somebody's back up.'

'Other writers manage to survive their books.'

'And I intend to survive mine,' he said with deceptive mildness. 'It's the people I care about that I can't protect.'

Her shoulders slumped as she heard the finality in his voice. 'I can't fight phantoms, Harry.'

'Nobody's asking you to.' He took a step forward but stopped when she flinched. 'This wasn't supposed to happen, Lisa. No matter what you think, I brought you here for your benefit.'

Tears coloured her voice. 'Don't do me any more favours, huh?'

Hardly seeing where she was going, she stumbled along the shell path towards the house. She was dimly aware that the storm had been building while they'd argued. The wind was a high-pitched whine, bending the trees almost double in its path. Leaves and debris flew through the air around her.

Before she had gone a dozen yards the first tropical raindrops splashed down on her head, quickly becoming a torrent which soaked through her clothes. In minutes she could hardly see the path for the intensity of the downpour. It was as if someone had turned a shower full on over her head.

Head down, she battled the mud which had turned sticky underfoot, her tears mingling freely with the rain. Damn Harry Blake and his precious principles. They might have been valid once, when he was an investigative journalist tackling dangerous assignments. But they seemed so futile now that he was out of the mainstream of his profession.

Into the fury of the storm she screamed her helpless rage. The sound was torn from her and lost among the chaos of other sounds as the seas pounded the island and wind and rain lashed the land.

Suddenly there was a great tearing crash over her head. She didn't see the tree limb which cracked through the branches on top of her. She only knew that the light was gone and the storm had stopped its banshee screaming.

CHAPTER FIVE

HARRY fixed his gaze on the turbulent sea, his thoughts equally chaotic. He wasn't being entirely honest with Lisa, even now. But hell, she hadn't given him any leeway and she was bound to misinterpret the truth.

Her accusation rang in his ears. Was he testing the strength of his resolve by bringing her here? If so, it hadn't been a conscious decision. After he'd found out that she was being harassed by that jackal Tyler Thornton his aim had been to protect her. It was his fault that she was in this fix, although she didn't know that either. A grin sloped across his face. He could imagine her reaction if she found out. She was really something when she was angry.

Easy, boy, he cautioned himself as the blood started to race and his stomach clenched with a familiar tightness. He meant what he'd told her about Kim. It was the last time anyone would get close enough to him to be held hostage to his beliefs.

He stood up and stretched his cramped muscles. Lost in thought, he hadn't noticed the rain starting and now he was uncomfortably damp. He'd better start back. With luck Lisa would have cooled down enough by now to see reason.

A faint cry brought his head up, his keen ears alert for the source of the sound. It was hard to pin-point above the gathering storm but he could swear it came from closer to the house.

'Lisa?' His cry mingled with the screech of the wind. But his feet were already moving over the shell path, heedless of the fallen branches strewn in his way. He leapt over a tree trunk the size of a telegraph pole. It had been torn out by its roots. He cursed himself as he ran. How could he have ignored the storm-warning signs and let Lisa head home alone?

He found her sprawled across the path a few yards from the house. At first he thought she was pinned under the torn branch covering her. But it moved easily aside. Under it she lay almost peacefully, her eyes closed and her lips gently parted on the cry which had summoned him. Blood was already clotting over a cut on her forehead. She was out cold but she was breathing.

She didn't stir when he checked her over, for which he was thankful. If anything was broken he would have had to hurt her. The thought wrenched at him with an almost physical impact but he pushed it aside. He'd deal with his own feelings later.

When he was sure nothing was broken he lifted her carefully and held her against him, where she nestled with a soft crooning sound as if she was aware of his attention at some unconscious level. He bent his head and kissed the wound on her forehead, then started for the house, stepping with infinite care so he wouldn't jolt her.

With the same care he placed her on his bed and pulled the quilt over her, then headed for the radio-phone, praying that the storm hadn't knocked out the system yet.

He was lucky. A static-laden voice answered his call. 'Is Alf there? I need him right away, over,' he said urgently.

'You hurt, boss?' Her concern penetrated the static.

'No, Rose, it's a friend of mine. Cut by a flying branch and possible candidate for concussion. She needs Alf's help, over.'

'No problem, boss. He's sleeping right here. It's time he went out and did some work.'

In spite of his tension, Harry chuckled into the handset. 'I'll tell him you said so. Over and out.'

He could picture Rose, a full-blooded islander, prodding her husband, Alf, awake. He had probably been up half the previous night delivering someone's baby halfway around the island. Harry hated to call him out during the storm, but as the only qualified doctor on the island he was accustomed to it and would chide Harry for doing anything else.

Alf Nawi and Harry had been friends since university and Alf had been delighted that Harry had chosen to drop out on his ancestral island. 'Do you good to pick up a bit of culture,' he'd assured Harry.

'Pick up some head-hunting and cannibalism, don't you mean?' Harry had joked good-naturedly. There was a grain of truth in it, however. Until the present century the people of the Torres Strait had been feared as pirates, head-hunters and cannibals. Alf's grandfather could well have been among them, although Alf himself was as urbane as any man.

Right now Harry wouldn't have cared if he'd been a witch doctor with bones through his nose as long as he could help Lisa.

A bright light shining in her eyes brought Lisa to full wakefulness. She struggled against the fingers gently lifting her eyelids. 'What happened? Who are you?'

She was lying on Harry's bed, she saw at once. A grey-haired black man, wearing nothing but a pareu tied around his waist and a pair of plastic-rimmed glasses, was bending over her.

Harry loomed over the man's shoulder. 'You were knocked out by a flying tree branch. This is Dr Nawi. He's making sure you're still in one piece.'

She struggled to sit up and immediately wished she hadn't as the room whirled around her. Harry rushed to place another pillow behind her head and she sank against it with a grateful sigh. 'Am I all right—er—Doctor?'

His teeth gleamed whitely against cocoa-coloured skin which contrasted with his crinkly grey hair and beard. 'You seem dubious about my qualifications. I'm afraid I left my medical degree back at my camp or I'd show it to you.'

'I'll vouch for him,' Harry said, resting a hand on the other man's shoulder.

She pressed a hand to her aching head. 'Where did you come from?'

'My camp is called Utingu, place of many big trees. It's beyond the spring, on the far side of the island.'

'Alf—Dr Nawi—is the elder of his tribe. He's the keeper of his totemic history, tender of cave paintings...'

'And healer of the sick,' Alf finished with a laugh. 'I decided my people needed my services more than yours did,' he told Lisa.

'Right now I'm not sure I agree with you,' she said shakily. 'My head is splitting.'

He nodded sympathetically. 'I'll give you something for the pain. Harry will need to keep an eye on you and call me if there's any sign of concussion.' His concerned gaze lifted to Harry, hovering anxiously beside them. 'Something tells me he won't mind having to spend the night at a young lady's bedside.'

Her colour heightened. The doctor thought that she and Harry were already sharing the bedroom. Apparently Harry's reluctance to share his life didn't extend to his bed, since his friend didn't seem to find her presence at all unusual. 'I'm sorry to be such a bother,' she said a little stiffly.

Harry frowned. 'I should have realised how bad the storm was getting, and made sure you got back safely.'

Instead of brooding about his own problems, she read into his statement. The doctor's puzzled glance went from one to the other, as if he sensed the undercurrents flowing between them. 'Luckily there's no serious harm done,' he said. 'Concussions are common enough at Utingu. People falling out of coconut trees and whatnot.'

'It sounds as if they keep you busy.'

'They do, considering we're only a small family group. I also travel to the outer islands when I'm needed, or they bring their casualties in to me. You must come and visit our camp,' he suggested, his dark eyes twinkling.

Her uncertain gaze flew to Harry. 'It's kind of you, but I'm not sure I'll be here long enough.'

'Long enough to let that cut heal,' the doctor insisted. 'Any larger and it would have needed stitches.'

She touched the square of adhesive bandage he'd applied to her forehead. 'I was lucky this time.'

The doctor wagged a forefinger at her. 'Next time you might not be so lucky, so let Harry keep an eye on you in future, eh?'

The prospect would no doubt thrill Harry, she thought sourly. The last thing he wanted was more responsibility for her well-being. He'd made his position clear at the look-out, which was why she was in this fix now. 'Harry's done more than enough for me already,' she said with heavy irony.

The doctor beamed at Harry. 'Not before time.'

'What did he mean by that?' she asked Harry after he'd seen the doctor on his way back to his camp, cautioning him to take care in the storm.

'Alf Nawi is a good Christian. He thinks everything should go two by two,' Harry said. It was obviously not a philosophy he shared.

'I gather you two are good friends,' she said, more to get him off the subject of togetherness than anything else. It also served as a distraction for the ache in her head.

'We were both scholarship kids at university. From first meeting Alf rode roughshod over every prejudice I'd ever had concerning Aboriginal people.'

'I didn't think you knew the meaning of the word,' she observed with a wry smile.

His eyebrow arched. 'Thanks for the vote of confidence, but I had my hang-ups like most other teenagers. Some of them I gave up voluntarily. Others had to be educated out of me.'

She couldn't resist it. 'All except one.'

His jaw tightened. 'Which one is that?'

'The streak of male chauvinism.'

Annoyance flared in his grey eyes. 'Now wait a minute; I'm not prejudiced where women are concerned.'

Softly she closed the trap. 'Yet you wanted to deny Kim the right to choose her own principles.'

'I'd deny anyone that right if it keeps them alive.'

'Then you would rob history of its greatest martyrs.'

With an explosive sound he turned on his heel and left the room. While she'd been talking to the doctor he had closed the louvred shutters against the storm, and she was left alone with their persistent rattling and the sighing of the wind in the rain forest.

She wasn't sure if she'd won or lost that round, or even if she really meant what she'd said about people having the right to die for what they believed in. On the other hand, if Kim had been an innocent victim it would have been different. But she was a journalist like Harry. Knowing the risks, she had urged him to write his story anyway. He shouldn't blame himself, yet he did.

Her thoughts chased around her tired brain like mice on a treadmill until the doctor's pills began to work and she drifted into a deep sleep. The music of the storm became a distant lullaby.

When she awoke sunlight streamed in through the open shutters. A pitta bird sat on the windowsill, chirruping its 'hello and wake up' call. She smiled at it dreamily then realised she wasn't alone in the room. Harry was slumped in a chair, his clothing rumpled and a dark smudge around his jawline suggesting he'd been there most of the night. His eyes jerked open as she sat up. 'Hello, Harry,' she murmured.

'How are you feeling?'

'Fine. A bit headachey, but that's all. I'm sure the doctor didn't mean you to take his suggestion literally.'

'I wanted to stay near by in case the house decided to become airborne.'

Her eyes widened. 'How much worse did the storm get?'

'If you don't count the cyclonic winds and the monsoonal rain, not too bad, I guess. We're still in one piece.'

She rested her head in both hands and groaned. 'To think I slept through the whole thing.'

He was at her side in an instant. 'Is your headache bad?'

The eyes she lifted to him were bright and clear. 'No. I just can't believe I didn't hear anything.'

'Alf's potion probably put you out. He wanted you to get a good night's rest.'

'Which is the understatement of the year.' She pushed the quilt aside and swung her legs over the edge, testing the extent of her recovery. When the room remained steady and the ache in her temples didn't increase she felt safe to stand up. Only then she realised she was wearing her white satin nightshirt. When she'd collapsed she'd been wearing her bikini. 'Did the doctor put me to bed?' she asked as suspicion dawned.

He yawned and stretched, massaging the dark line along his jaw. 'I wasn't aware it took a medical degree.'

He was laughing at her! 'It doesn't, but it usually requires the person's permission,' she fumed.

'Last night you were in no condition to give me permission to do anything—and I mean anything,' he said with maddening accuracy. 'So relax, will you?'

It was difficult when she was acutely aware that he had seen all there was to see of her. She had to admit she was also just the tiniest bit piqued that

he didn't seem impressed by the experience.
Perhaps, compared to some of the women he'd
known, she was a disappointment. She pulled
herself up short. After his warning she wasn't
interested in impressing him, was she?

'Thank you for taking care of me,' she said, re-
sisting the urge to grab the quilt and swathe it
around herself. She was the one bothered by her
scant covering, not him.

He nodded. 'It was the least I could do. I
shouldn't have let you go off by yourself in a storm.'

It was more than she could stand. 'It wasn't your
fault,' she yelled at him. 'You aren't responsible
for everything that happens to me.'

Before he could respond she stormed into the
bathroom and showered away her frustrations,
taking care not to wet the bandage Dr Nawi had
put on her head.

The storm, the flying branch and Harry coming
to her rescue seemed like a lifetime ago. Had she
dreamed it or had Harry really kissed her when he'd
carried her into the house? Maybe it was her own
wishful thinking, prompted by a hit on the head.

'How soon can we go back to TI?' she asked
over a light breakfast of melon and toast.

The stubble was gone but shadows rimmed his
eyes as he looked at her. 'Missing Simon?'

She hadn't given Simon Fox a thought for a
whole day. It was Harry himself she needed to get
away from. Knowing how she felt about him, when
there was no future in it, was becoming more than

she could tolerate. 'I wouldn't want to outstay my welcome,' she said.

Over the rim of his coffee-cup he regarded her steadily. 'You don't have a choice. The storm pushed my boat up on to the beach with a hole in the side you could drive a car through.'

'There must be other boats on the island.'

'There's one at Utingu, but I wouldn't borrow it unless it was an emergency.'

'But this is——'

'Just because you can't wait to get back to your precious Simon doesn't make it an emergency,' he growled, forestalling her. 'My boat is fixable. It'll only take a couple of days and some tools I loaned to Alf Nawi. Would you like to come with me to fetch them back? He did invite you to visit their camp.'

Her spirits sank lower. He was only inviting her because the doctor would expect her to accompany him, not because he wanted her along. 'How far away is the camp?' she asked, curious in spite of herself.

'About an hour's walk through the rain forest,' he told her. 'If you aren't up to it I can postpone it for a few days.'

The sooner he retrieved his tools, the sooner he could fix the boat and return her to TI. Her headache had almost gone. It was probably due to lack of food as much as anything. She hadn't eaten anything since yesterday morning and the breakfast was making all the difference. 'I'll be fine if we take it slowly,' she assured him.

When they set off she was horrified at the extent of the storm damage to the island. Uprooted trees lay strewn across the paths like discarded toys. Pools of rainwater steamed in the morning sun. They would be gone by afternoon, Harry told her. Where the path skirted the beach she saw great ribbons of seaweed pushed well above the usual high-water mark. Debris littered the sand like the aftermath of a gigantic under-sea picnic.

'I hope Dr Nawi's people are all right,' she said when they stopped to rest.

'That's another reason why I want to get there. The storm blew my aerial down, so I couldn't radio to find out how they coped.'

The gruffness in his voice betrayed his concern. 'You really care about these people, don't you?'

'They're my people, too. Alf and I became tribal brothers after we graduated.' As she opened her mouth to speak he gave a warning shake of his head. 'Don't ask for details. Alf's people are touchy about what men and women may know. In his father's day women were killed for sticking their noses in where they didn't belong.'

She gave a low whistle. 'And I accused you of being a male chauvinist.'

His lop-sided grin did peculiar things to the pit of her stomach. 'Let's say I'm a people chauvinist. Does it help?'

'Maybe.' She was unwilling to admit it, but it helped a lot to know that he had such compassion for the traditional owners of the island. His closeness to Alf Nawi and his obvious respect for their customs earned her admiration. Added to his overpowering maleness, it made a formidable combination. She was thoughtful as they set off again.

A tree root caught at her ankle and she stumbled. A firm hand clamped around her elbow and steadied her. 'Are you all right?'

'Yes, thanks. Well, maybe a little shaky. How much further is Utingu?'

'Just over this ridge. You can rest there while I round up my tools. If I know Rose they'll insist on inviting us to lunch before we head back.'

'Rose is Alf's wife?' He nodded and she went on, 'They won't expect me to eat witchetty grubs or raw goanna, will they?'

'They may offer you some traditional food but they won't be offended if you refuse. On the other hand, you might surprise yourself and like it. As a travel agent I thought you'd be more adventurous.'

'I am adventurous,' she assured him. 'But I have this aversion to eating anything I've been introduced to first.'

His hearty laugh echoed around the rain forest. 'Remind me not to catch any mudcrabs or crayfish for you while you're here.'

He was teasing her, and the idea pleased her inordinately. 'I love seafood, provided we haven't met,' she repeated. 'If it makes me a hypocrite I can't help it.'

His eyes darkened and his grip on her elbow tightened. 'You could never be a hypocrite,' he denied. There was something frighteningly attractive about the way he was looking at her.

She drew a strangled breath. Under the canopy
of green his face loomed awfully close. Her lips
parted in an instinctive gesture and she licked them.

'Little Lisanko Nikitayevna,' he murmured,
drawing out the syllables as if they were words of
love.

Her parched throat closed on the words. 'Nobody
calls me that any more.'

He ran a finger around her jawline. 'They should.
It's a beautiful name.'

She could feel the soft wind of his breath on her
upturned face. 'You make it sound beautiful. Oh,
Harry, why must we fight all the time?'

'Maybe because it's safer than the alternative.'
He released her and plunged off into the rain forest.

She ached to call him back, to finish what he'd
started, to ravish her lips and plunder her body the
way she wanted him to do, had thought he was
about to do when he'd looked at her in that
smouldering way.

But he was right. There was no point starting
something they couldn't finish. If it hadn't been
for the storm, she'd be on her way back to TI by
now and they both knew it. It must be the aftermath
of her accident which was making her so vul-
nerable today.

They emerged on to a chalk-white stretch of sand
against which the Arafura Sea rolled endlessly. Far
down the beach, a woman cast a net into the surf
and pulled it back in a fluid gesture. The net was
alive with tiny sardine-like fish. Harry told her that

the dark drifts of what looked like seaweed floating offshore were massive schools of these fish.

'So many of them?'

'It's a land of plenty, which is why visitors to the island need the permission of the traditional owners to come here.'

It was a measure of the respect the islanders held for Harry that they had sold him part of the island, she realised. 'How do they feel about tourists coming here?' she asked.

'They agree, provided the group is small and the people respect local customs,' he said. 'Alf is wise enough to realise that his people need a source of income for the things the land won't provide, such as medicine and a wider education.'

Her eyes shone as she pictured the scene. 'The visitors can learn from Alf's people, too. They could try their hands at traditional skills such as fishing and net-making, hear the dreamtime legends and learn about the cave paintings...' Her voice slid away on a sigh. 'It is what you had in mind, isn't it?'

Amusement sparkled in his grey eyes. 'It's exactly what I had in mind, which is why I want you to organise the visits; no one else.'

She felt a guilty surge of understanding. Simon would want to build huts along the beach and run a fast catamaran service from TI to Drummer Island. The huts would appear to be primitive, of course, in keeping with his image of providing holidays off the beaten track, but they would be modern and comfortable inside. Simon knew his market well.

But there was also a segment which wanted to experience places like Drummer Island as they really were, even if it meant enduring slight discomfort. To them the island would be paradise exactly as it was.

How unspoiled it was. The beach, at least a mile of it, was a pure French grey with a rocky point at one end which gleamed whitely with shells. Where they'd emerged from the rain forest was the mangrove-fringed mouth of a stream which threaded the sand with silver.

Nestled among towering coconut palms was the village itself, or camp as Alf Nawi called it. The houses were built in traditional style of bamboo and palm fronds with beaten sand floors. Diesel generators supplied the villagers with power.

A fishing net strung between two trees provided a swing for the children. It was deserted now, and the sing-song voices coming from a hut told Lisa the children were at school. It was a charming mix of the new and the old.

Alf Nawi came out to meet them. Trailing shyly behind was a mahogany-skinned woman who bared uneven white teeth in a warm smile. 'Hey, Harry! Good to see you, boss.'

He embraced her. 'Good to see you, too, Rose.' He took a step back and included Lisa in the circle. 'This is Lisa Alexander.'

'How your head today?' Rose asked, touching a gentle finger to the bandage adorning Lisa's forehead.

Lisa was charmed by her concern. 'It's fine, thanks to your husband's care.'

Rose gave a dry laugh. 'Him only doctor. Harry the one you need to take care of you here.' She pressed an expressive hand against her heart.

A change of subject was urgently needed. 'The village doesn't seem to have suffered any storm damage,' she observed. For some reason this set Rose off into gales of laughter. Lisa shot Harry a helpless look.

Into her ear he murmured, 'Rose can't understand why you're being so coy about our relationship.'

'We don't have a relationship. That's crazy,' she whispered back.

He gave a lop-sided shrug. 'They're much more open about sexual matters than we are. As they see it, for two healthy adults *not* to have a relationship—now that's crazy.'

She was about to dispute the point when he gripped her elbow hard. 'When in Rome, Lisa.'

While her Western upbringing urged her to set the record straight part of her saw his point. What did it matter if Rose and Alf thought they were—or should be—a couple? She tried to relax in his grasp. 'You're right. As long as we know the truth.' At least there was no uncertainty there.

A furrow appeared between his eyes as if she had angered him in some way. 'Of course,' he said curtly. 'Now maybe you'll stop defending your honour long enough to enjoy my friends' hospitality.'

The nerve of him! She was only following Harry's own rules. Apparently his friends didn't know about his rule against getting involved.

She pushed her annoyance aside as Rose took her hand and began to show her around the village. It was home to about fifty people, most of them related. Soon Lisa had met Rose's brother, Ernest Tamoy, his wife, Amy, and several younger relatives. They all welcomed her with the same gentle warmth, taking it for granted that she 'belonged' to Harry.

Several times she had to bite her tongue to keep from blurting out that she didn't belong to Harry because he didn't want her to. According to Alf's people, everyone had to belong to someone. All young girls were betrothed before they were out of childhood, although they didn't live with their husbands until they were of marriageable age.

Gradually Lisa began to understand how foreign her single status appeared to them. No wonder they took it for granted that she and Harry were a pair. To them it was the natural and proper order of things. She saw now why Alf had said her arrival was not before time.

In the centre of the village chickens pecked at split coconut halves, and Rose threw them handfuls of grain in passing. They provided the villagers with almost their only source of fresh meat. Everything else came from the sea or the rain forest.

The tour over, Lisa was urged to sit beside Harry, adopting his crosslegged pose on palm-frond mats. This was the moment she had dreaded, when she would have to eat a traditional meal of who-knew-what.

Harry saw her swallow apprehensively and squeezed her hand. Lisa hastily withdrew when she heard Rose's tongue-clucking noise of approval.

She needn't have worried. The islanders had inherited a mix of Aboriginal and Polynesian cultures, so there were no witchetty grubs or raw goanna on the menu. Lisa had no trouble coping with fish baked on hot coals and eaten with the fingers from palm-leaf plates. Succulent mangoes, coconut meat dug from the husk with seashell knives and date-like fruit called wongai completed the meal. Rose smiled as she handed Lisa the dried wongai fruit.

'You like wongai?' she asked.

'It's a cross between a plum and a date, only more subtle,' Lisa mused aloud. 'Yes, I like it.'

'Good, good.' Rose seemed pleased with herself.

Oh, no, don't let it be a fertility thing, Lisa prayed, catching on at last. Harry saw the quick flaring of anxiety in her expression. 'Relax; local legend says that if you eat the fruit of the wongai tree you are destined to return to the island,' he explained. 'The seeds are used in jewellery and are highly prized for wood-carving.'

Relief almost obscured the real significance of the fruit. How could she return where she wasn't wanted?

The meal ended with a local treat called *pisang rimpi* which turned out to be preserved strips of banana dried in the sun. Fresh spring water washed the meal down.

The doctor had been quiet during the meal, content to let his wife do most of the talking. Now he stood up. 'Would you like to visit the cave of our ancestors, Lisa?'

The sun was already low in the sky but excitement stirred in her. 'I'd love to, although won't it be too late to see the paintings properly?'

Alf smiled indulgently. 'Not these paintings. They're intended to be seen at sunset. Aren't they, Harry?'

Harry seemed suddenly uncomfortable. 'Lisa isn't completely recovered from her accident. Maybe she would rather go there some other time.'

'I'm perfectly all right,' she said defiantly. Who was he to make her decisions for her, even if Alf's people believed he had the right? 'I'd love to see them,' she said, shooting him an acid look. 'Where are they?'

'Harry will show you,' Alf said, sitting down again. 'The place is known as the cave of lovers.'

CHAPTER SIX

'I TRIED to warn you,' Harry said as he led the way out of the village.

Prickles of apprehension travelled down her spine. 'Warn me about what?'

He glanced back, his face impassive. 'The cave of lovers is the local equivalent of the honeymoon suite.'

Suspicion took root in her brain. 'What are we expected to do there?'

'What do you normally do in a honeymoon suite?'

'Oh, no.'

'Oh, yes. Alf's been angling to get us up here ever since he set eyes on you. If you'd let me do the talking I could have convinced him you weren't well enough to visit the cave, but you had to contradict me.'

'I was only going along with local custom, as you asked me to do,' she defended herself.

He grabbed an overhead branch and swung himself around to face her. 'No, you weren't. You only insisted on going because I said you didn't want to.'

Now they were both stuck with the consequences. It was obvious that Harry hated the idea, but she had put him in an impossible position. He couldn't refuse without offending Alf's people. She scuffed the toe of her sandal in the leaf litter beneath the tree. 'I didn't realise what was going on. I'm sorry if I made things difficult for you.'

'Not for me, for us,' he contradicted. 'A honeymoon takes two, remember?'

As if she could possibly forget it when his closeness threatened to overwhelm her. The rugged lines of his face were deepened by the dappled shade. With one hand gripping the branch overhead he looked primitive and dangerous. And she was following him to a pagan place of betrothal.

'Maybe we could go back to the house by another way,' she whispered, her voice strained by the tension gripping her throat.

'Alf would know about it before we got a dozen yards from the village.' He released the branch with a snap which ricocheted along her taut nerves. 'Is that how you show respect for their customs?'

Desperation lent power to her voice. 'Respecting their customs is one thing, but participating in them is quite another.'

His eyes turned luminous in the late-afternoon sunlight. 'You were the one who volunteered for this.'

Knowing he was right shattered her remaining resolve. It was worse admitting that she'd done it to prove to the villagers that she didn't belong to him in their sense of the word. If she hadn't been so pig-headed none of this would have happened. 'I did, didn't I?' she said so softly that it was barely audible. 'So what are we going to do now?'

'What we're expected to do. Visit the cave of lovers.'

Conflict surged through her. What they were doing was madness, given the way she felt about him. He didn't want to share the cave with her, yet she'd left him no choice. If she went along at least he would retain the respect of the local people. Whatever it cost her, she owed him no less. 'I'll go,' she agreed.

He offered her his hand to negotiate the steep path which wound between pinnacles of eroded rock. At last they reached a curtain of tree roots which concealed the opening to the cave. Pulling aside the roots, Harry motioned for her to enter.

'It's amazing.' The admission was torn from her by the sheer size and spectacle of the place. The cave was no more than twenty feet deep from front to back, but the roof disappeared in shadow overhead. The entrance was strewn with ceremonial shells and small bones, and every inch of the walls was etched with designs, some so faint that they must be thousands of years old.

The most noticeable feature of the cave was a platform at the deepest point. About twelve feet square, it was made from bamboo poles with dried branches laid across it. At first she thought it was some kind of altar; then heat raced through her as she realised what it was. 'A bed?'

'I'm afraid so.'

Averting her eyes from it was difficult since it was the only furnishing in the cave. She concentrated on the drawings covering the walls.

On closer inspection they weren't a good choice either. 'I didn't know the Aborigines went in for erotic art,' she gasped, realising what the many stick figures portrayed.

'This is *puri-puri*, wish-fulfilment art,' he explained. 'It's drawn to achieve a purpose, such as bringing a particular woman to your bed.'

Her throat dried and waves of heat travelled along her limbs but she couldn't tear her eyes away from the drawings. Some were no more than crude stick figures, hastily drawn before the artist could be discovered at work. Others were in the X-ray style and were nothing if not detailed. She eyed the designs with awe. 'They're so... so...'

'Explicit?' His voice so close to her ear made her jump. His approach had been cushioned by the thick carpet of sand across the floor of the cave. 'They spell out tribal marriage customs and laws.' His finger traced the lines of a grossly distorted figure. 'These ones broke the laws and suffered for it. They're called Quinkans and they're supposed to live in the crevices in the caves.'

Her eyes roved around the cave as if seeking the spirit people. 'Some of the paintings must have been here for centuries, yet they look freshly drawn,' she said on a shiver.

'Alf and his sons are responsible for touching them up regularly. He's the custodian of this cave.'

'I'm surprised I'm allowed to look at them,' she said with a shaky laugh which showed what a dubious privilege she thought it was. 'Didn't you say there are laws about what men and women may see?'

'There are, but Alf believes you have a legitimate reason for being here. Our presence serves the purpose of the cave, so the spirits aren't offended.'

Her own feelings for Harry certainly qualified, but she wasn't at all sure about his for her. More than ever she wished she had held her tongue in camp. Her legs felt weak suddenly, and she sat down on the edge of the platform. It felt surprisingly soft and yielding. For the first time she noticed blankets piled at the foot of it and a kerosene lamp on top. At least they would have light for the vigil ahead.

When she pointed the items out to Harry his mouth thinned. 'I should have realised what Alf was up to all along.'

She touched his arm. 'It's all right. I don't mind, honestly.'

His mouth curved into a wry smile. 'Maybe Alf is more perceptive than I realised.'

Her heart almost stopped as he regarded her with a warmth which kindled answering fires along her veins. She could feel her pulse-points throbbing and her heart set up a hectic tattoo in time with them. This must be how a bride feels on her wedding-night, she thought in astonishment. The cave was getting to her. She was reacting as if they were really here to consummate their relationship. She put a hand to her whirling head. 'Oh, dear.'

He dropped to his knees beside her. 'What is it? Headache? Blurred vision?'

Hysterical laughter thrummed through her. He thought her reaction was caused by the cut on her head. What would he say if she told him she had been picturing their wedding-night? She let her hand slide to her lap. 'This place takes some getting used to, that's all.'

'If you feel ill we don't have to stay. Even Alf would understand that.'

It was tempting to clutch at the offered straw. Maybe Harry would prefer her to accept it as a face-saving way out, but the lie froze on her lips. Did she want an excuse to spend the night with him? Was she hoping to inflame him with passion until he changed his mind about her? If so it was a stupid, childish thought and she pushed it away. 'I'm all right,' she insisted.

He unwrapped a parcel he'd taken from among the blankets. 'Maybe you'll feel better if you eat something.'

She was instantly wary. 'Eat what?'

'They've left us some dried fruit and nuts.' He showed her the parcel. Among the pieces of banana and pawpaw were several dried fruit from the wongai tree. 'I think I detect Rose's hand in this,' he said wryly.

She accepted a piece. 'Maybe she's trying to tell us something.'

Some of the tension dissolved as they exchanged smiles of understanding. In her own way Rose wanted to ensure that Lisa returned to the island. They ate in companionable silence, then Harry lit the lamp and fetched plastic cups of spring water from a pool near the cave mouth. He handed one to her. 'What are you thinking?'

'What a wonderful place this is for visitors. I know they can't come into the cave proper, but there are plenty of other things to interest a small group.'

His heavy sigh punctuated the silence. 'The venture should be a great success.'

The edge in his voice surprised her. 'I thought you liked the idea.'

'I do, but this place is designed for more romantic thoughts than your next business venture.'

Her stomach knotted as the tension returned. 'I understood that romantic thoughts are off-limits where you're concerned.'

'I said permanent involvements are off limits.'

'But not flings, casual liaisons, one-night stands?' Try as she might, she couldn't keep the hurt out of her voice.

'I admit that celibacy doesn't hold a lot of appeal,' he said, his voice falling to a husky baritone. 'But I'm sure I'll manage to last the night, so there's no need to sound so panic-stricken.'

Some of the fight ebbed out of her, but whether with relief or disappointment she wasn't sure. She wanted Harry to make love to her more than she had ever wanted anything, but she was also old-fashioned enough to want it to mean something to both of them. It promised to be a long night.

As soon as darkness closed in the rain forest came alive with squeaks, chirrups and the flap-flap of wings. 'Fruit bats; they won't hurt you,' Harry assured her when she instinctively drew closer to him

on the platform. The lamp isolated them in a pool
of flickering light. All else was darkness. Even the
silvery moonlight seemed to keep a respectful distance from the cave.

She didn't object when his arm slid around her
shoulders, recognising it as a gesture of comfort.
But flames leapt through her at his touch. The
eddies of cool air whirling around them seemed
charged with the spirits of those who had used the
cave to seal their bonds of love.

How wise these people were! The darkness was
like velvet and the isolation so complete that they
might have been the only two people on earth.
Adam and Eve.

She wondered what Harry would say if she linked
her arms around his neck and brought his magnificent head down to her breast. Excitement stirred
inside her and she moved a little away to still the
frantic beating of her heart. The need to be loved
beat at her as a pulse-pounding tattoo flaring along
every nerve pathway to her brain.

She tried to tell herself she was lonely. Apart from
one heart-stopping affair at university, which had
petered out as soon as the man had found out about
her parents, her experience of love was limited. The
cold war had made all things Russian immediately
suspect, including her. The world had changed since
then but she hadn't dated seriously, except for
Simon, and he seemed to find her background
fascinating.

Her one-sided love-affair with Harry at nineteen
didn't count precisely because it *was* one-sided. But

it was still the most shockingly powerful taste of human emotion she had encountered.

She sneaked a sideways glance at him. The planes of his face seemed carved from granite, his eyes deep pools of mystery. The tension he radiated made her fairly certain he was regretting their situation. 'I'm sorry,' she whispered, touching his hand.

Her touch galvanised him. Pin-points of light radiated from his pupils as he stared at her. 'You're sorry? For God's sake, why?'

'For getting you into this.'

'It's too late to change things now.' His voice was gravel-harsh. 'I could make it back in the dark but you'd probably break your charming little neck.'

Her sharply indrawn breath made him relent. 'Cheer up, Lisa, it's only for one night.'

It was the kind of tone he'd used when she was a teenager, to convince her that what she felt for him would pass. The hurt he'd inflicted still reverberated inside her. She hadn't known about Kim then, of course. Would it have made a difference? 'I suppose we should try and get some sleep,' she suggested diffidently.

'I'll stay awake for a while longer; otherwise I'll be wide awake at two in the morning.'

She sighed, reminded that he wasn't keen to share the bed with her on any basis, even the most platonic. 'You're right. I'm the same if I go to sleep too early.'

He settled his back more comfortably against the curved sandstone wall, chuckling sardonically. 'Then we'll sit up and talk.'

Her laughter meshed with his. 'It isn't exactly what Alf Nawi had in mind, is it?'

'Hardly.' He paused thoughtfully. 'I shouldn't have accused you of not respecting his customs. Not many women would put up with these conditions with such good grace.'

'It's not so bad,' she said, meaning it. She had never been so totally alone with a man before. Every nerve-ending felt sensitised. Where it would lead she wasn't sure, but she knew she didn't want it to end yet. Another thought occurred to her. 'Fitting in with Alf's people isn't so hard. I had lots of practice at fitting in while I was growing up.'

'Moving around so much with your parents?'

She shifted restlessly as painful memories surfaced. They seemed more poignant here somehow. 'We moved house about every two years before we finally settled in Cairns. Mama couldn't accept that they were really free.' She gave a self-deprecating laugh. 'As a bonus I pick up accents quickly. No matter where I go, I can manage to sound like everybody else in no time.'

'You had much more of a Russian accent as a teenager,' he observed. 'Where did it go?'

'I only had it around Mama and Papa. Part of my verbal chameleon act.'

In response to the bitterness which threaded her voice his hand slid over hers. 'Yet you never learned to speak Russian.'

The contact stilled some of her agitation. 'Papa didn't want me to. He spoke it with Mama, whose English was never good, but they wanted me to be completely Australian.' Outwardly they had succeeded, but inwardly part of her reacted like a frightened refugee, panicking at the sound of a knock late at night.

He sensed her inner turmoil. 'Our parents always want a better life for us than they had themselves. My father was the same. He was a foreign correspondent and hardly ever at home. After my mother died he put me into a boarding-school, thinking I'd have a more stable background. I was eight years old.'

Her heart went out to the lonely little boy he must have been, even as she saw his point. Like her parents, his father had done the best he could. 'Yet you became a journalist yourself,' she commented.

His grin flashed whitely in the darkness as if she had touched a nerve. 'Not without putting up a fight. I tried the law first, but I met so much injustice in the legal field that I was driven to speak out. My betters suggested that lawyers should be impartial. I wasn't, so I got out.'

'Do you ever wonder what your life would have been like if you'd had an ordinary childhood?' she asked, voicing her own deepest concerns.

He gave a throaty chuckle. 'You could never have been ordinary.'

Just as he could not have kept silent on issues which troubled him, she realised. She shifted uneasily. 'You make it sound as if we have some kind of destiny.'

'Alf would say we do. For myself I think we're given the raw materials to mould our own destiny.'

His mention of Alf reminded her of the reason they were here. 'I suppose Alf would be disappointed if he could hear us waxing philosophical.'

His hand felt warm in hers. 'I doubt if he'd understand. Not that he professes to understand much that our people do. He thinks we're an illogical lot.'

As his fingers moved under hers a fresh wave of tension gripped her. 'What will you tell him tomorrow?'

There was a pause. 'Nothing. What he thinks is another matter.'

She gulped. 'Alf and Rose...they'll think that you and I...that we...' What had happened to her flair for languages now?

'That we're betrothed,' he finished for her. 'I'll be lucky if I can stop him from laying on a wedding feast and painting you in ochre and emu feathers.'

Horror-struck, she wrenched her hand from his grasp. 'He wouldn't!'

'Relax, I was joking. Except about the ochre. Traditionally the bride is painted in some very fetching places, to make her more alluring to her husband.'

She couldn't tell whether he was joking or not. The *puri-puri* in the cave must be affecting her, for she felt waves of heat washing over her. Her limbs were molten, yet her skin was cooled by the breezes wafting in through the mouth of the cave. How could she be hot and cold at the same time?

He touched her arm with the back of his hand. 'You're shivering. Let's get under the blankets.'

Her self-control was already stretched to the limit, whether with the effect of the cave or her imagination running riot. She shook her head. 'I'm not sharing that thing with you.'

'It's too cold to sit up all night.'

'I'm not sleepy yet,' she denied.

His lop-sided shrug was parodied by his giant shadow sloping off one wall of the cave. When he shook out the blankets the shadow reached giant hands for her and she shrank back involuntarily.

He stretched full-length on the platform and pulled the blankets over him, opening one corner in blatant invitation. She looked away.

For the next half-hour she fixed her gaze on the cave mouth, wrapping her arms around her bent knees against the chill seeping into her bones. When his breathing slowed she decided to risk joining him under the blanket. Her limbs were like ice. If she sat up any longer he'd have to chip her off the cave wall in the morning.

Gingerly, trying not to disturb him, she kicked off her sandals and slid under the blanket, keeping as much of the platform between them as the skimpy covering permitted. Congratulating herself on achieving her objective, she snuggled gratefully into the warm cocoon, only to come to rigid attention as an arm eased across her middle, the fingers resting beneath the curve of her breasts.

She could have sworn he was fast asleep. 'Harry?' she said tentatively.

'Darling.' His voice was so soft that the word came out almost as a sigh. Yet she was sure she'd heard correctly. She closed her eyes as his caress seared her to her core. Pressing her hand over his, she drew him harder against her, transmitting the relentless rhythm of her heartbeat to him through her T-shirt. In response his fingers tightened over the sensitive cusp of her breast, until eddies of pleasure whirled through her.

'I love you,' she murmured into the darkness. What did it matter if there was no tomorrow for them? Today was all anyone ever had. Harry must be thinking similar thoughts, to have abandoned his vow not to make love to her.

Five years of waiting exploded inside her as raw, driving need. Thinking gave way to action as she melted against him, linking her hands behind his head to draw his mouth down to her. When their lips met desire so exquisite that it was almost painful speared through her. 'Love me, Harry,' she implored, cupping his face with her palms.

He clasped her closer, making her thrillingly aware of his love-hardened body. 'Kim,' he murmured thickly. 'Kim, darling.'

Her limbs turned to ice and shock waves reverberated through her. What had he called her? He said something more but it was inaudible. He *was* asleep and thought she was Kim.

He moved against her and the embers of her passion flared until she doused them with a jolt of reality. The need to be loved still throbbed through her, making her shudder at the thought of what she had so nearly done. She had told herself she was willing to accept his love on any terms, but they didn't include being a stand-in for another woman.

With robot-like movements she inched to the edge of the platform and huddled there, out of his reach. When he rolled on to his side away from her she bit her lip hard on a cry of anguish. Trying to convince herself that it was better this way helped a little, but she was still wide-eyed when the first light of morning slanted across her face.

No more than two hours had passed between closing her eyes and Harry touching her shoulder. 'Time to get up.'

Her body was stiff from holding herself away from him. The night was over. It was about the only thing she felt thankful for.

He offered her a slice of freshly harvested mango. 'Want some breakfast? I picked it myself.'

She averted her eyes. 'No, thanks, I'm not hungry.'

His keen gaze raked her face. 'What's the matter, Lisa?'

She couldn't hide her distress. 'Last night you tried to make love to me.'

'I was asleep, but you obviously don't regard that as an excuse.'

'The cave affected both of us,' she said stiffly. 'I didn't exactly try to fight you off.'

'Is that why you're upset? Because you feel you betrayed Simon?'

The derision in his voice made her vision blur. 'Simon has nothing to do with this.' She kept her voice level with an effort. 'While you were...touching me...you called me Kim.'

He spiked his hands through his hair. 'Bloody hell. No wonder you're upset. I don't suppose I can say anything to improve matters?'

She shook her head. Not even sure why she needed to know, she asked, 'Did you ever bring her here?'

'I didn't know the place existed then.'

It was some small consolation. He tried to touch her shoulder but she shrugged him away. 'Don't, please.'

'Very well. But you must know I didn't mean to hurt you. I was asleep, for goodness' sake.'

In a sense so was she. Asleep to reality and dreaming of things which could never be. She stood up, brushing twigs from the platform off her clothes. Her skin felt sticky and unpleasant, but she would have to wait until they returned to the house to shower and change. 'Can we go back now?' she asked dully.

He cast the remnants of the fruit into the forest. 'I'll collect my tools from Alf and we'll be on our way.'

She endured the villagers' rather ribald teasing with resigned good humour. Their gesture was well-meant. It wasn't their fault if it had backfired. She was relieved when Harry retrieved his tools from Alf Nawi and announced that they could leave.

The doctor insisted on checking the cut on her head, replacing the gauze bandage with a smaller flesh-coloured one, before farewelling them with more gentle teasing. His wife stayed in the background, her smug smile betraying her satisfaction at fulfilling her role of matchmaker. If she only knew, Lisa thought as she followed Harry along the beach path.

'What will Dr Nawi think when he finds I've left the island?' she asked to break the strained silence.

Harry's expression was impassive. 'He's a man of infinite patience. No doubt he'll wait for you to come back.'

There was a catch in her voice as she said, 'Then it's a shame I'll have to disappoint him.' She quickened her steps before he could see the tears filling her eyes at the thought of leaving.

Harry was at her side in two strides. 'Can't you forgive a man for one little mistake?'

More angry than she had ever been, she rounded on him. 'Little mistake? You fondled me and then called me by another woman's name.'

His winning smile eroded some of her anger. 'Which are you objecting to?'

He was laughing at her! 'Damn you to hell, Harry Blake. This isn't a game, at least not to me.'

His fingers gripped her upper arms and his expression sobered abruptly. 'It isn't to me, either. Last night got to me, too. Being in the lovers' cave with you was like being shown a beautiful vision then realising it isn't for you.'

He drew a deep breath then let it out slowly. 'I wanted you very much last night, Lisa. I think I conjured up Kim's name to stop myself from doing something I knew we'd both regret later.'

Through the tears which clouded her vision she asked, 'What makes you think I'd regret it?'

His jaw muscles tightened. 'If I were Simon Fox I'd make darned sure you regretted it.'

Bitterness drove her to retort, 'Then I'm thankful you're not Simon. At least he gets my name right.'

Tearing herself from his grasp, she blundered away through the rain forest, only dimly aware of where she was going. Right now it didn't seem to matter whether she ended up in the ocean. Then the spring came into sight. She was almost back at the house. Harry hadn't rushed to follow her, she noticed, setting her jaw more firmly. What did she expect from someone who was still in love with a ghost?

CHAPTER SEVEN

'WOULD you like something to eat?'

Lisa shook her head. The atmosphere between them was still strained. It was an effort to keep her tone civil, but she reminded herself that Harry had warned her. She couldn't blame him because her one-sided fantasy lay in ruins. 'All I want right now is a shower and change of clothes,' she told him.

'Then you use the bathroom first. I want to check on the aerial, so I'll shower afterwards.'

While she soaped herself under the stream of tepid water she heard him working above her. He whistled as he did so and the sound increased her sense of isolation. By the time she was finished and dressed in her sundress he was in the kitchen, making sandwiches.

'I'm taking these down to the boat with me,' he informed her. 'Sure you don't want some?'

She eyed the doorstep-sized wedges of bread and filling with distaste. 'No, thanks. I'll make something later if I'm hungry.'

'You aren't coming down to the boat with me?'

More than anything she needed some time to herself to come to terms with what had happened in the cave. 'No, I need to make some notes about Alf's village, see how it can be worked into a package to interest a select group of visitors.'

His shoulders rose and fell. 'Suit yourself. You know where to find me if you need me.'

'How long do you think the repairs will take?'

Tension crept into his features. 'Anxious to get back to your friend?'

She tossed her head in a defiant gesture. 'I thought you'd be happy to have me off your hands.'

'Common sense tells me I should be,' he muttered darkly.

Which hardly answered her question. She spread her notebook and pens out on the table. He started for the door, turning as he reached it. 'If you want to use the radio it's operational again.'

As his footsteps retreated down the shell path she dropped her pretence of working and rested her chin in both hands. He thought she wanted to call Simon, but the idea hadn't crossed her mind. She supposed she should call him, if only to tender her resignation.

Visiting the village had helped to crystallise her ideas on how the island's tourist potential could be developed. She saw herself setting up a tour company specialising in the Torres Strait islands and the tip of Cape York. She even had a name picked out—Island Idylls. Setting it up would take most of the money she'd invested from the sale of her parents' house, but it was a risk worth taking.

From her experience of working with Simon she knew there were plenty of tourists who wanted to see the real Australia. They would eat the local foods, sleep in palm-frond huts and learn the

legends of the Dreamtime from Alf Nawi and his
people.

Chewing on a pencil, she recalled a sign she'd
seen somewhere in the outback: 'Take only photos,
leave only footprints.' It would become the golden
rule on Drummer Island. She wanted it to remain
unspoilt and magical.

Despite Harry's concern, she wasn't worried
about leaving Simon. He would be angry at her defection, but she was sure he didn't love her any more
than she loved him. The novelty of having a minor
celebrity on his staff appealed to him, and he
wouldn't welcome her as a competitor, but it was
time she tried her own wings. One of Simon's
regular clients, a rich woman who'd taken every
package tour on their books, had started pestering
him for a job to relieve her boredom. The woman
would fill Lisa's shoes easily. In more ways than
one, if Lisa knew Simon.

The only stumbling block was Harry himself. Not
about the tourist project. He was as keen to see it
succeed as she was. But escorting groups to the
island would mean seeing him on a regular basis.
Could she cope, knowing the future held no promise
for them? Knowing she loved him, she added with
a strangled sob. There was no point hiding the truth
from herself any longer. Last night had proved
beyond doubt that he was the only man she would
ever love.

Unconsciously she straightened her back and
took a deep breath. If she left now the future certainly held nothing for them. But if she was under

Harry's eye every few weeks who knew where it might lead?

The thought infused her with a fresh burst of creative zeal. She could hardly write fast enough to capture the ideas spilling through her mind. Island Idylls began to take shape, on paper at least.

The radiophone crackled to life, breaking her concentration. Harry had shown her how to answer it, so she flicked it on and gave his call sign.

The response chilled her with its unexpectedness. 'Tyler Thornton here, calling from Brisbane. Who is this, over?'

She thought frantically. How had Tyler Thornton managed to track her down. 'Uh, this is Rose,' she said, giving the first name which popped into her head.

'Oh, yes, the village woman. Harry's mentioned you. Is he there, over?'

'No, he's down at his boat.' Darn, she should have made her English sound less precise.

He was too preoccupied to notice. 'Well, tell him to get back to me right away. I've been trying to call him for two days. He must have the evidence he promised me by now. Did you get all that, Rose?'

'Oh, yes, I got it all right.' In shock, she wrote down the telephone number he gave her, then signed off. For long minutes she clutched the handset in nerveless fingers, then she dropped it as if it could bite. Harry was working with Tyler Thornton.

How could she have been so gullible as to think that Harry would protect her against one of his own kind? She remembered her earlier thought: once a journalist, always a journalist. It seemed it was true.

No wonder Harry hadn't wanted to make love to her at the cave. He only wanted her here to provide the missing link between Tyler Thornton and his story. Maybe the whole tourist venture was a lie too, dreamed up to keep her occupied and unsuspecting.

She was hardly aware of the tears streaming down her face as she tore out of the house and along the shell path which led to the beach. She had promised to give Harry the message and, by heaven, she would do it.

He was fitting planks along the damaged side of his beached cruiser when she reached him. His mouth was full of nails, which he hammered into a plank before he acknowledged her presence. 'You decided to come down after all. Good, we can have a picnic when I finish this.'

The dinghy he used between cruiser and shore was also drawn high up on the sand, and she kicked it in fury. 'I didn't come down here for a picnic.'

He lowered the hammer he'd been wielding and looked at her, his face shadowed by his broad-brimmed straw hat. 'What is it? What's happened?'

'I just received a call from Tyler Thornton.'

He rested his tools on the deck and pushed his hat far back on his head. 'Given his resources, he was bound to find out where you were sooner or later.'

Bitterness fuelled her laughter. 'Resources such as a friendly man on the spot, don't you mean?'

His eyes narrowed. 'You'd better say what *you* mean, Lisa.'

'Isn't it obvious? You didn't bring me here to protect me from Thornton, but to try to get the information you both want by another method. What was the deal—you got the girl and he got the story?'

'It would make sense if I *had* gotten the girl. As I recall, nothing happened.'

'Yet,' she threw at him, her voice thick with pent-up emotion, 'if you hadn't slipped up and called me Kim it probably would have done.' Clasping her arms around herself in a defensive gesture, she stared far out to sea, blinking hard to clear her vision. 'When you told me about Kim I understood. I even grieved with you. I could see your need to keep things casual between us. I told myself it was beautiful and noble. But it isn't beautiful to find out you've been used.'

He reached for a rag and wiped his hands with jerky movements. 'Nobody's using you, Lisa, least of all me. You know how much I care about you. If you'll just let me explain.'

His eyes lifted, inviting her trust, but she was beyond listening to explanations. She clapped her hands over her ears. 'I've heard all the sweet talking from you I can handle. When I was nineteen I loved you, really loved you. I thought you were the most wonderful man ever to walk the earth. Then you left and I thought I was the one with the problem, that you couldn't love me.

'Today, I started to hope that maybe...just maybe...we might have a future if I was patient and let you see that love doesn't always turn out the way it did for you and Kim. Now I find it's all a hateful lie.' Her voice cracked and she faltered, having said far more than she had intended to. Horrified with herself, she backed away. 'Fix that thing, will you, so I can get out of here?'

His expression underwent a sea change from reasonable to blindly furious. With a mighty sweep of his arm he knocked the tools off the deck and into the shallows. 'Since you won't listen, what's the point of continuing this? If you want the boat fixed, fix it yourself.'

Something snapped inside her. He had betrayed her and now he wouldn't allow her to leave with what dignity she could muster. 'Traitor,' she yelled at him. Blinded by fury, she swung her head from side to side. The sea had become her prison, with no way out unless he chose to allow it.

Well, she would show him. Before he could move she had dragged the dinghy down the sand to the water and threw herself into it.

'What the hell are you doing? Come back here!'

Words weren't going to stop her. She scrabbled for the oars lying in the small boat, and thrust them into the row-locks, missing one and having to try again. When she had them in place she began to haul on the oars to move the boat, anywhere as long as it was away from this island.

Progress was slow, and she became aware of Harry standing knee-deep in the shallows, his hands planted on his hips as he watched her with ill-concealed annoyance. The sight gave her a moment of grim satisfaction. As far as she knew he didn't have another boat, and his cruiser was laid up, so he couldn't stop her.

It wasn't until she reached the centre of the lagoon and the drag on her arms reminded her of how far it was back to the mainland, that sanity began to return. She couldn't possibly row all the way to Thursday Island, and there was nowhere else to go, except to crawl ignominiously back to Harry.

This thought made her set her jaw more firmly. To hell with Harry. There had to be another way.

Suddenly the boat began to rock alarmingly, tipping from side to side with such force that she had to grab the sides to avoid being tossed into the water. Her first terrified thought was of sharks, but there were none inside the coral reef and she hadn't yet crossed it. Then the boat almost turned over and she was dumped into the water, tumbling down and down until she collided with the sandy bottom.

She choked on salt water, struggling to reach the air above. Hampered by her skirt, which clung to her legs, she put all her strength into kicking for the surface. Before she reached it strong arms clasped her and lifted her head above water.

'You bastard,' she gasped as she saw what sort of predator had tipped her out of the boat. She rained blows against his chest in helpless frustration. 'You tried to drown me.'

His legs pumped powerfully beneath her, supporting them both. 'I saved you from drowning,' he said calmly. 'Another few yards and you'd have been across the bar. The sea could have swamped your boat, then you'd have been shark bait.'

'Oh, God.' Reaction gripped her and she sagged against him. He didn't seem to mind and clasped the back of her head, pulling her tight against his chest. Whorls of wet chest hair teased her cheek, sending up flares of response all the way to the centre of her being.

Confusion swamped her. Here was a man who had betrayed her then tried to drown her, ostensibly for her own good. Yet she was responding to him like Juliet to Romeo. She must be mad, sex-crazed, anything but sane and sensible.

With his arm across her chest he began to tow her back to shore. 'What about the boat?' she asked, trying not to notice the disturbing effect his movements were having on her peace of mind. Held so close to him, she was disturbingly aware of every masculine muscle and contour. His wet clothes clung to him like a second skin, outlining every rippling movement. She swallowed hard. Where was her will to escape now?

'The tide will wash the dinghy back in,' he said, his breathing deep and even as he guided them through the shallows.

She struggled ineffectually in his grasp. 'I can swim the rest of the way on my own.'

'I didn't go through this to lose you now. Relax and trust me, if only this once. And, for crying out loud, shut up. I can't talk and swim at the same time.'

It was a strange sensation, relaxing in the crystal-clear water which was as warm as a bath, allowing Harry to do all the hard work. Tufts of seaweed drifted by, small silvery fish nibbling at their edges. At the beach they disturbed a manta ray, which rose majestically in a puff of sand and winged its way out to sea.

What had she expected to achieve with her crazy gesture? She hadn't really intended to row back to TI and there was nowhere else to go. Had she wanted Harry to come after her and save her from herself? If so she was a blind, stupid fool. He was in league with Tyler Thornton and no amount of grand gestures altered the fact.

So why did her heart persist in pounding like the surf against the shore when he placed her gently on the sand? It couldn't be exertion. He had done all the work. So it had to be the intoxicating way his gaze held hers as he loomed over her. When his mouth sought hers there was a dizzying inevitability about it, and she gave herself up to the sweet sensation.

Instead of kissing her his mouth hovered over hers, tantalising her. 'What are you doing?' she whispered.

'You nearly drowned. I'm giving you mouth-to-mouth resuscitation.'

About to remind him that drowning victims were usually unconscious, she throttled the words back. It would be a terrible waste, not to be able to savour every moment of her own rescue. The thought made her part her lips expectantly.

At the blatant invitation his breathing quickened, and he bent his head, puffing small breaths into her mouth. The sensation was unbelievable and turmoil roiled inside her. This wasn't a kiss. It was pure seduction. She ran a tongue around suddenly dry lips.

His remaining control snapped and he crushed her mouth under his as his fingers traced the line of her jaw and throat with eager, mind-numbing caresses. Her fingers dug into his back and she moaned softly, drowning now for sure, but in quite a different way.

Desperately she tried to think of all the reasons why this was wrong, but none of them came to mind. They were blanked out by the irresistible hunger of her need for him. The feeling was so powerful that it rocked her to her foundations. No more could she deny it than she could have rowed all the way back to Thursday Island.

He made a crooning noise deep in his throat, raining kisses over her brow and eyelids until she was on fire with wanting him.

'Harry, please,' she pleaded. Somehow it came out as an invitation.

'I know, love, I know.' He buried his face in the curve of her shoulder. She gasped as his teeth nipped the silken skin, then he pushed aside the straps of her sundress to expose her unfettered breasts to the golden sunlight. His hands moulded them until her nipples strained against his palms.

When he kissed first one, then the other, wildfire tore through her. She pressed her mouth to the top of his head, cradling his neck while he inhaled her feminine essence. His chest was hard against her, slick with sea-water and salt residue, and the rough feel of it sensitised her skin in a thousand places until she was one mindless, quivering mass of sensation.

An urgent warning rang in her brain. 'Say my name, Harry,' she implored, hearing her own voice sounding passion-drugged and languorous. But there was no mistaking the urgency of her request.

He lifted his head and his slitted gaze slid over her. 'Lisanko Nikitayevna Alexandrov,' he drawled, sounding out each syllable with husky precision.

Her soft sigh of contentment rippled between them. This time he knew exactly who she was. 'Just checking,' she murmured.

Mock anger sparked in his eyes. 'In that case, I should do a little checking of my own.'

Her sodden dress was twisted around her hips. He bit his lip as he carried out his own inspection of her tanned limbs, sprawled wantonly on the sand. His throaty murmurs told her he approved of what he saw.

She made herself lie still until he had completed his inspection, kissing each part of her to seal his approval. 'Do I pass?' she asked as his lips trailed down her legs, sending waves of pleasure shooting along her spine. It was hard to believe he could arouse her with a look, but his minute inspection managed it somehow. She was on fire by the time he finished.

'You'll do,' he said with a lazy grin which didn't quite conceal his own excitement. His eyes burned and his heart raced when she pressed her hand to it. With a throaty exclamation he grabbed her hand and guided it lower until she was left in no doubt as to his response to her.

The reality of Harry as her lover eclipsed her wildest dreams. He was more tender, more passionate, more dominant and more inventive than she had dreamed. The powdery sand cradled them as gently as a couch while the waves lapping at their feet created a whole new range of sensations.

She clung to him wildly, blindly, driven by his passion and her own desperate need. He was driven, too, she saw, holding himself back only by a mighty effort of will until he sensed that she was ready to soar with him on a joyous climactic surge of abandonment.

When it came her eyes widened with shock and wonder. Nothing in her experience had prepared her for this. The roaring of the sea mingled with that of the blood in her ears, then there was blackness.

Seconds later she surfaced to find Harry painting butterfly kisses along her hairline. 'Did I pass out?' she asked, bewildered.

'It's been known to happen,' he murmured against her ear.

Alarm spun through her. 'Does that mean there's something wrong with me?'

'It means there's something very right. I've never
known a woman like you, Lisa. You're something
special.'

He propped himself up on one elbow. The tide
had risen slightly and the water lapped around their
ankles. She cupped her hands behind her head and
looked up at him. 'I came down here to fight with
you,' she reminded him, her tone tinged with
wonder.

His lazy grin warmed her. 'Madam, I do like the
way you fight.'

Reality was beginning to seep back as steadily as
the rising tide. 'You know what I mean. I hate the
thought of your working with Tyler Thornton.'

He grazed a finger along the curve of her hip,
making a mockery of her seriousness. How could
she think straight when his touch threw her thoughts
into chaos? He saw the flicker of annoyance on her
face and withdrew his hand. 'I'm not working with
Tyler Thornton,' he said heavily. 'But I did give
him the tip-off which started this whole thing.'

She sat up, shedding droplets of sea-water. 'You
what?'

'It's a long story. Maybe we should go back to
the house.'

'Maybe we should.' As she stood up she was
aware of how her waterlogged dress clung to her
body, outlining every curve. Normally she would
have felt self-conscious under his gaze. Now she
was too preoccupied with what he'd just said. How
could he make love to her, knowing he was the cause
of her problems? He probably needed the walk back

to the house to come up with a convincing
explanation.

As he bent to retrieve his shorts she noticed the
red marks of her fingers on his shoulders. Shame
flooded through her. She couldn't even blame his
silver tongue for what had just happened. She had
wanted it every bit as much as he had. Her mistake
had been in thinking of it as a beginning when, to
Harry, it was an end in itself.

Back at the house, she showered quickly, aware
as she sluiced herself down of the heightened sen-
sitivity in her body. Her skin felt raw, her nerve-
endings electrified. She should be appalled at her
own lack of restraint, but instead she felt released
from a tension which had been building inside her
since she'd encountered Harry again on Thursday
Island. Who was it who'd said that the best way to
get rid of temptation was to yield to it?

She had certainly yielded to it, she thought with
a hollow feeling. She had never behaved so recklessly in her life. And now to find out that Harry
had put Tyler Thornton on her trail.

If she'd possessed wings she would have flown
away from the island rather than face Harry again.
It was too humiliating to accept that she had let
him make love to her on any terms, even knowing
he was tied up with Thornton. What sort of woman
did that make her?

He was much more composed by the time he'd
showered and changed into a fresh pair of Stubbies'
shorts. Still no shirt, and her senses leapt at the
sight of his bronzed chest, remembering the feel of

his rough hair against her cheek. Her eyes travelled to where the shorts rode low on his hips, and she felt colour creep up her face as she looked quickly away.

'Not regretting what we did?' he asked, observing her reaction.

'Of course I am,' she snapped back. 'You've already admitted that you set me up by bringing me here. How could I have let myself...?' She couldn't go on. Her hands flew up to cover her face.

With an oath he wrenched them away. 'Look at me, Lisa. I did not, repeat, *not* set you up with Thornton or anyone else.'

'Then what did you mean about tipping him off?'

'Exactly what I said. When I was researching your father's biography I left some notes in my computer at the newspaper where I was working. They weren't supposed to be accessed without my password. Thornton was working on the same paper and somehow got into my files. The story he's chasing now was triggered by what he learned.'

She curled herself on to a wicker chair, pulling her legs up underneath her. 'Why did he wait so long to do anything about it?'

'There was no point pursuing it at the time. Your parents were the only ones who knew the full story, and they would never talk to the likes of Thornton.'

'So what has changed since then?'

'Information is much easier to get out of Russia nowadays. He can follow it up more easily. But, most importantly, your mother had the only proof that the story was true.'

'The mysterious photo,' she said on a sighing breath.

He nodded. 'The photo. Thornton believes that you inherited it, and he wants to get his hands on it.'

An involuntary shudder shook her. 'So you agreed to help him get it from me?'

His hands clamped on to her shoulders and he shook her slightly. 'I did *not* agree to help him. I let him think I would so he'd leave you alone.' He took a step back, his fingers stabbing through his damp hair which curled across his forehead like an inverted question mark. 'I felt responsible for getting you into this. It was the only way I could get you out of it.'

An arctic wind of despair swept through her. Guilt had prompted him to bring her here. He blamed himself for her predicament and wanted to make amends. It wasn't the romantic scenario she'd allowed herself to fantasise about.

'Now do you believe me?'

She gave a hollow laugh. 'Oh, yes, I believe you. In fact, it makes a lot of things much clearer.'

His hard gaze bored into her. 'It has nothing to do with what happened just now, if that's what you think.'

Now she knew he was telling the truth. Making love to her had been an isolated event, fuelled by the needs of the moment—which was precisely why she felt so bereft. The only face-saving way out was to be as casual about it as Harry was being, pretend it hadn't mattered any more to her than it had to him.

'Don't worry,' she said, keeping the hurt out of her voice. 'I'm not one of Alf Nawi's people. I don't consider us engaged just because of a quick fling on the beach.'

Her choice of words made him wince. 'You have changed, Lisa.'

Her hurt came out as anger. 'It's more than I can say for you. The story's still the most important thing, isn't it? Obtained by fair means or foul.'

'I did not make love to you to get information,' he ground out, his grey eyes sparking with anger.

'I know.'

He regarded her suspiciously from under lowered lids. 'Why do I get the feeling that there's more to this?'

'Because there is. I saw the manuscript in your room, remember? *The World's Best-Kept Secrets*, isn't it? One of them wouldn't be my mother's, by any chance?'

'Yes, it would, but——'

She didn't give him chance to finish. 'So you decided to beat Tyler Thornton to it. I believe the correct journalistic term is scoop him.'

She held her breath. More than anything she wanted him to deny it so that she could believe that he was truly protecting her from the other journalist. 'I was going to write about it, yes,' he admitted after a long pause. 'But only because Marya wanted the story told. She wanted me to write it after her death, precisely so it wouldn't be distorted by the likes of Thornton. Why do you think your father wanted his biography written by me?'

'So it wouldn't be sensationalised afterwards,' she echoed, remembering Nikita's reasoning. Knowing that Harry was carrying out her mother's last wish didn't lessen the hurt of how he had used her. 'Why didn't you tell me about the book?' she asked.

'Would you have come with me if you'd known?'

'No.'

He spread his hands wide, palms upwards. 'I intended to tell you as soon as I was sure you'd understand.'

'Oh, I understand all right. If Thornton gets the story first your book isn't worth anything. But you're both going to be disappointed. There is no photo and no scoop. I don't even know what this is all about.'

He pulled a chair closer to her and crossed an ankle over one knee. His closeness set her pulses racing but she damped them down. She'd been as weak as she intended to be where he was concerned.

'There isn't a lot to tell, but it's time you heard it,' he began. 'Does the name Lyudmila Duskov mean anything to you?'

CHAPTER EIGHT

'LYUDMILA DUSKOV was related to the Russian royal family. When the tsar and his family died in 1917 she was only a child, but because she posed a threat to the regime her name was changed, and she kept quiet ever after. Her name stays in my mind because my mother's sister had the same first name.'

'She had the same last name as well, Lisa.'

'Are you saying she *was* my aunt?' When Harry nodded she shook her head. 'You're wrong. My aunt's surname was Chekhov.'

'Lyudmila Chekhov didn't exist until your mother came to Australia,' he said evenly. 'Did Marya ever talk to you about her sister?'

'No, and I didn't press her because it upset her so. In any case, Lyudmila died before I was born.'

'On the same day Lyudmila Duskov died, unknown in her own country and to the world. Doesn't that strike you as coincidental?'

'But why would Mama keep it a secret? Wasn't she proud of her sister?'

'More proud than you can imagine. It's precisely why she didn't want their relationship becoming public. So she put Chekhov as her maiden name on the papers she was given when she came to Australia.'

He spun the chair around and straddled it. The pose strained the fabric of his shorts over his muscular thighs and she swallowed hard. It was difficult to keep her mind on the past when the present kept intruding so insistently.

She fixed her eyes on his grave expression. 'What does this have to do with Tyler Thornton?'

'He knows about the link between Marya and Lyudmila and he wants to make it public.'

A voice of protest rose inside her. 'Just the sort of headlines Mama wanted to avoid.'

'I'm afraid so. Thornton isn't big on scruples when he senses a juicy story.'

Her lashes dropped over moist eyes. 'Would it be such a big story now, with both Mama and her sister gone?'

'Of course it would. The photo showed your aunt surrounded by the royal family. Think what the Press would make of that—and of you, too, and your "royal" relations!'

In spite of herself, a slow smile seeped across Lisa's face. It was an odd feeling to think of having relatives, when she'd grown up with none. Then her expression grew pained. 'Why did Mama tell you and not me?'

'She had no choice. I stumbled on the photo when I was going through your father's papers. When I tackled Marya about it she allowed me to delve into the story, provided I kept it secret during her lifetime.'

'Surely the photo isn't the only record of their relationship?'

'It's the only one we have access to, which is why Thornton wants to get his hands on it.'

She was still confused. 'Why did he wait so long?'

'My guess is that the story didn't interest him until he found out I was working on a book. He and I crossed swords many times when we worked for the same paper. He probably sees this as the perfect way to get even, and make some money at the same time.'

Her hair had dried and fluffed around her head. She ran distracted fingers through it. 'How can an old photo be valuable?'

His eyes darkened. 'Scandal is always valuable. The more famous the person it attaches to, the higher the price the media is prepared to pay. Which is why we have to stop Tyler Thornton getting hold of it.'

So that Harry could use it first in his book, her tired brain supplied the rest. Once a journalist, always a journalist, she reminded herself silently. To him the story was all-important. If she needed one his wife's death was a tragic reminder. 'Why didn't you tell me all this when I arrived?' she asked, her tone accusing.

'I had my reasons.'

She tossed her head defiantly. 'Such as wanting the photo for your book?'

A grim expression crossed his face before the shuttered look returned. 'Such as wanting you to enjoy the island, free of shadows from the past. Once you found out about the photo I knew you'd look at me the way you're doing now, as if I'd just crawled out from under a rock.'

She hadn't realised that her feelings were so transparent. But he was wrong about one thing. Her look of loathing wasn't for him so much as for herself. Despite his warnings, she'd allowed him to make love to her, fooling herself that it could mean anything to him.

'I don't hate you, Harry,' she said evenly. 'One thing my parents taught me was the futility of hate. I am sorry that you weren't honest with me.' Unable to contain her restlessness, she jumped up and paced to the window, leaning far out to inhale the cleansing perfume of the rain forest.

When she had mastered her turbulent emotions she whirled on him. 'Was it all true about Kim, or did you exaggerate the story to gain my co-operation?'

His breath whistled out between clenched teeth. 'God, no. The whole thing's on record if you want to check.'

She gave a wry smile. 'I shan't bother. Crazy as it seems, I trust you.'

'You know I wouldn't hurt you for the world.'

Perhaps not, but he would mislead her then charm her into behaving so recklessly that she squirmed to remember it. The thought of their bodies entwined on the sand made her writhe with mortification. She had known of his involvement with Thornton when she'd confronted him on the beach, yet she had still allowed him to make love to her. Worse still, she had enjoyed it so much that her body ached to feel his touch again. He had called her a fever in his blood, but he was an addiction to her. She shivered involuntarily.

'What will you do now?' he asked, regarding her intently.

The slow burn of anger caught her by surprise. 'I'm going back to Cairns to turn my flat upside-down until I find that photo.' The hard planes of his face didn't alter but she sensed his growing tension. 'If I find it I shall destroy it,' she finished flatly.

Reaction flickered in his gaze. She had expected fury but was startled to see something very like respect in his eyes. Then it was gone. 'You can't destroy the truth, Lisa,' he told her.

Disappointment knifed through her. She had been hoping he would approve of her decision. It would mean that she was more important to him than the story. Would she never learn?

'I have to try,' she went on. 'I can't take any more of this media tug of war around me. For once I want to be an ordinary person. Not the daughter of Nikita and Marya Alexandrov, but plain old Lisa Alexander, daughter of Nick and Mary. Can't you understand what it feels like to grow up as a media freak show?'

His lip curled derisively. 'Poor little Lisa. Are you telling me you never once used your background to get something *you* wanted?'

'I didn't...' she began, then couldn't meet his eyes any longer.

'Never?' he drawled. He swung his leg over the chair and joined her at the window. His touch on her arm was light but irresistible. Her head came up. 'What about your present job?'

She squirmed uncomfortably. 'I didn't want Simon to use my background. It was his idea.'

'It's what I expected. I'll bet he makes sure your clients know who they're dealing with?'

She nodded miserably. It was a bone of contention between her and Simon that he had mentioned who she was in a local Press release when she was hired. When she'd asked him outright if it was the reason why she'd got the job his evasiveness had answered her question. Yet she hadn't resigned.

'And what about your father's share of the book proceeds which you inherited?' Harry went on relentlessly. 'Don't you regard it as tainted money?'

'No,' she said, her voice almost inaudible.

'You can't have it both ways, sweetheart. It's no use blaming the media for exploiting you unless you're prepared to send the cheques back.'

His palms crossed in a slashing movement. 'Hell, Lisa, we all have problems with our family history. It's up to you to make the best of what you are instead of railing against it. Self-hatred will get you nowhere.'

In spite of herself, she was forced to concede that he made sense. All her life she had longed for the anonymity her school-friends enjoyed. Running away from Tyler Thornton and threatening to de-

stroy the photo if she found it were the latest steps
in a pattern of running away.

'And another thing,' he continued, pressing home
the advantage he sensed he'd gained, 'but for who
you are, I would never have met you.'

She managed a shaky smile. 'Under the circum-
stances, maybe it would have been a good thing.'

'No.' His denial cut through the air like a whip-
crack. 'Don't even think it. I wouldn't have missed
knowing you for the world. I hope you feel the
same.'

Would it ease his conscience if she did? The fact
was she couldn't feel as casual about sex as Harry
could. Lines from a poem danced into her mind:
'man's love is of man's life a thing apart, 'tis
woman's whole existence'. Try as she might, she
couldn't make it 'a thing apart'.

All the same, she couldn't regret what had happened either. No matter what sort of woman it
made her, she was glad—joyously, recklessly glad—
that she had known Harry's love. If it was all they
ever had she intended to hug it to her like a guilty
secret for as long as memory endured. Her shy smile
reflected this secret knowledge. 'No,' she admitted
with absolute candour, 'I wouldn't have missed
knowing you for the world.'

His eyes searched her face. 'No regrets?'

Those she had were for the future, not for the
past. 'Not about what happened,' she confessed.
Before he could probe deeper and reveal how fragile
her assurance really was she asked him, 'What will
happen if the photo never comes to light?'

'Thornton's story falls flat, and there's a hole in my book,' he said.

'Would you mind?'

His slow grin gave her the answer she needed. 'There'll be other books.'

Her spirits soared. Maybe he was telling the truth when he said he wanted her on his island for her own sake. She began to hope the photo would never resurface.

'Hungry?' he asked.

Suddenly she was. Determined to enjoy their remaining time together, she volunteered to cook. While Harry harvested fresh salad vegetables, she grilled thick slabs of barramundi fish from Harry's freezer.

After dinner they took their drinks out to the terrace and sat admiring the canopy of stars which seemed close enough to touch. In the distance the sea became a flaming band of reflected light, gathering ribbons of pink and gold from the sunset sky.

The night sounds no longer frightened her. The flapping noises she recognised as the leathery wings of the fruit bats as they wheeled across the sky, dipping down to drink from the freshwater spring.

When it was fully dark clouds of ghostly luminescence drifted across the landscape. Harry told her they were fireflies. To her they looked like Christmas fairy-lights. She hoarded the sights and sounds greedily, wanting to be sure she could conjure them up again when she returned home.

Home. A pang shot through her. Where was home now? It should have been her flat in Cairns.

Now she wasn't sure. Since coming here she'd undergone some sort of emotional transplant. The idea of leaving wrenched at her. It meant leaving Harry. She hoped that when the time came she would have the strength to make a graceful exit.

As the silence lengthened Harry regarded her with concern. 'Are you sure you're all right, Lisa?'

Her smile was forced but convincing in the shadowy light. 'I'm fine. I have a lot on my mind, that's all.'

'Your aunt, you mean?'

In truth she'd hardly given what he'd told her about her aunt a thought. It was a relief to know why Tyler Thornton was interested in her, but it hardly made a difference to Lisa herself now. She had more pressing concerns.

When she kept silent he stalked to her chair and dropped his hands lightly on to her shoulders. The touch electrified her and it took every ounce of will-power not to show it. 'I think I know what's on your mind,' he said in a soft voice.

'You do?' Her reply was revealingly high-pitched.

He was behind her, so she couldn't see his face, but she heard the anxiety in his voice. 'When we made love I wasn't thinking too clearly. I didn't do anything to protect you. But if anything comes of it I want you to know that you can rely on me. I won't let you down.'

Despite the evening's warmth, a chill shook her. His charity didn't extend to an offer of marriage, she noticed. Bitterness threatened to choke her.

'You needn't worry; there's no chance of my becoming pregnant.'

He should have been relieved but he seemed angry as he moved away. 'I should have realised, because of you and Simon.'

Harry couldn't know it, but her confidence stemmed from fortunate timing, not from any precautions she'd taken on Simon's behalf. He was more than willing to deepen their relationship, but so far she'd resisted, instinctively knowing that he wasn't the man for her.

That man was right here beside her, but he might as well have been on the moon for all the good it did her. Maybe she should give Simon another chance. At least he wanted her.

She stood up. 'It's been a long day. I'm going to bed.'

'Goodnight, Lisa. Sleep well.' He had retreated into the shadows, his voice sounding world-weary. He didn't follow her when she went inside.

For what seemed like an age she lay under the mosquito netting, staring into the darkness and wishing fervently for sleep. When it came she dreamed of being chased by men with miniature tape-recorders which they kept thrusting into her face, demanding information.

More and more of them besieged her until she could hardly breathe for the howling mob pressing in on her. Suddenly they were flung aside like broken dolls and a path opened in front of her. In the centre of it stood Harry, his commanding figure haloed by light. He held out his arms to her.

As she moved towards him the light intensified until she threw an arm across her eyes to shield them. When she pulled it away the dream dissolved into the fierce light of the morning sun, shining full into her eyes.

A muffled sound caught her attention. Instantly she became aware of another presence in the room. Jolting upright, she thrust the netting aside to greet the spectacle of Harry riffling through her luggage. 'What are you doing?' she demanded.

He straightened. 'I didn't mean to wake you.'

'Obviously not. You're looking for that photo, aren't you?'

'Finding it is the only way to make Tyler Thornton leave you alone,' he said.

She bit her lip so hard that she tasted blood. 'Funny, but he isn't the one going through my things.'

He gave an impatient shake of his head. 'Would you have agreed if I'd asked permission?'

'Asking never crossed your mind. At least be honest with me this once, Harry. You want the photo as much as Thornton does, not to protect me but to score journalistic points off a rival.'

'Is that what you think I'm doing?'

'Isn't it obvious? You said yourself that you two have old scores to settle. All this stuff about setting the record straight is a convenient cover—admit it.'

The burning anger in his face caught her by surprise. Muscles worked in his throat and his hands clenched tightly at his sides as if he would like to lash out at someone. 'I'm delighted you have such a high opinion of me, Lisa.'

Her own anger was more than a match for his. 'Well what do you expect—undying gratitude?'

His eyes blazed. 'Hardly. But trust would be a start.'

'I did trust you and this is the thanks I get.'

With a sob she pulled the covers over her head to blot him out of her sight. The oath which split the air shocked her rigid. With words as his stock-in-trade Harry normally didn't need to swear. But why was he so angry? It could only be because she had caught him in a dishonourable act and he didn't like it. She heard him say something about going to work on the boat, then he slammed out of the house.

Slowly she lowered the sheet and used a corner to blot her moist eyes. She had been fooling herself that she could transfer her affection to Simon. If only she could! But how could you give away something which already belonged to another? Whether or not the gift was welcome made absolutely no difference.

She was shaking as she got out of bed and pulled on a shirt and jeans. She hardly glanced in the mirror as she pulled a comb through her tousled locks then threw the comb across the room. What was the point of taking pains with her appearance when there was no one to appreciate the result?

Her eye fell on the small silver-framed photograph of her parents on their wedding-day. It was one of the few personal possessions they had been able to carry out of Russia, and Lisa treasured it as a rare link with the past. It accompanied her everywhere. Now she picked it up, gazing into Marya's madonna-like face under the antique lace head-dress.

'Why didn't you tell me about Aunt Lyudmila? You told Harry.' Her mother's expression remained frozen in bridal serenity. 'You could at least have told me where to find the photo, then none of this would have happened.'

Suddenly she missed her parents more than at any time since they'd died. Pain clutched at her and she thrust the photo back into her bag. Hungry, she was hungry.

In a daze, she stumbled to the kitchen. Emptiness gnawed at her. There must be something here which would fill it.

Frantically opening and closing cupboards, she piled food haphazardly on to the counter-top. Bread and butter, cheese and jam, dried fruit, biscuits and tinned goods were dragged out.

She took bites of bread, a sliver of ham, some dried apricots and a spoonful of ice-cream. Then she began to assemble a sandwich to rival Harry's doorstep variety. Mayonnaise. It needed mayonnaise.

She chewed on dried apricots while she hunted through the shelves until she found the mayonnaise, then added a dollop to the sandwich before cramming more bread on top.

More ice-cream jarred her teeth before she was ready for the *pièce de résistance*. She had taken her first huge bite from the sandwich before she realised what she was doing. Horror flooded through her. Suddenly the food felt as if it were choking her and she rushed to the sink to rid herself of it.

For long moments she stood at the sink, numb fingers gripping the cold metal edges while she fought to control the heaving in her chest.

No amount of food would assuage the hunger gnawing inside her. Trying to eat away her problems would only destroy her health and appearance, as they had so nearly done in her teens. Recovery had needed both counselling and painfully acquired self-knowledge. What was she doing, throwing it all away now because her foundations had been shaken?

It came as a shock to discover that her old insecurities were so near the surface. She couldn't even blame Harry. She had let him think that she took his lovemaking casually, too proud to admit that Simon wasn't her lover. And Harry had warned her about getting involved with him. Putting his story ahead of her feelings was natural to him. He couldn't know that it had almost destroyed her.

Trembling with reaction, she gulped a glass of water to wash away the medley of sweet and savoury tastes from her mouth, then spun out of the kitchen. If she looked back she was lost.

It was time to be honest with Harry, she told herself as she hurried down the shell path towards the beach. Even if he threw her feelings back in her face, she had to tell him. No matter that he didn't

want her love. Some things were beyond personal
choice or control.

The cruiser had been repaired, and rose at anchor
a short way out in the lagoon, she noticed as she
passed it. Soon Harry would be able to take her
back to Thursday Island for the journey home to
Cairns. The thought made her more determined
than ever to catch up with him.

He was loading fishing gear into the dinghy at
the far end of the beach. Shading her eyes with one
hand, she saw him push the boat away from the
shore, then jump aboard. 'Harry, wait,' she called
but the sea breeze carried her words away. He didn't
even look up.

By the time she reached the spot he was a good
twenty feet from the shore. Gritting her teeth, she
waded after him.

He saw her and swung the boat around, his
expression set. 'What do you think you're doing?'

'I'm coming with you.'

'Are you, now? After your judgement of me this
morning I'm surprised you want to be on the same
ocean with me.'

Nevertheless he helped her to clamber aboard.
Her jeans dripped sea-water into the boat, and she
wrung the bottoms out ineffectually. 'I want to
apologise for what I said,' she began.

'You're entitled to your opinion.' He wasn't going
to make this easy for her, she thought as he steered
the boat towards the reef guarding the entrance to
the lagoon.

'Are we going outside the lagoon?' she asked as apprehension gripped her. At any other time he would have considered her fear of the ocean, but today he was much too angry to accommodate her.

She decided to wait until he started fishing before she said her piece. He rowed with such punishing intensity that she knew he was working off his anger. He didn't even notice the way her fingers gripped the sides of the boat as fear began to take hold.

The ocean was so huge and this was such a small boat. With two of them aboard they were frighteningly close to the water. It was an effort to tear her eyes away from the white-capped surface, and her stomach began to heave in tune with the rolling waves.

Since she was here without his invitation, she couldn't very well ask to be taken back, so she gritted her teeth and waited him out.

He anchored just outside the reef, where the sandy bottom abruptly shelved. On one side was the reef, and the other dropped away into darkness. As Harry laced the water with fragments of bread, fish clustered around the boat, mouths open and brown eyes rolling like beggars waiting for handouts. She was glad Harry was the fisherman. Much as she enjoyed eating fish, she didn't think she could hook one of these human-looking creatures.

She focused on the flowering cliffs of coral which rose enamel-bright out of the shallow side. A travel brochure in her files said that the Great Barrier Reef was the world's largest living thing, covering a distance as large as England, Wales and Ireland together.

Where the reef came close to the surface anemones danced like underwater willows, their long tentacles streaming like fawn and purple hair blown on submarine winds. No wonder the Greeks had named them 'daughter of the wind'.

'Lisa, hold on!'

She tore her eyes away from the coral to see Harry's fishing line streaming away from the boat at lightning speed. Fear clutched at her as she caught sight of a slanted dorsal fin curving off above the surface of the water. A shark had taken Harry's line.

He slashed at the streaming nylon with his knife, then hauled on the oars. She clung to the boat with all her might, a prayer hovering on her lips.

Suddenly something hit the boat with tremendous force. The boat skewed madly. Braced for another attack, Lisa bit back the scream which clogged her throat. She had never known such blind terror but she knew that, somehow, Harry would get them out of this.

Her eyes went to his face. He was white and his mouth was set in a thin line as he fought to control the boat in the boiling wake of the shark's strike. They were almost at the entrance to the lagoon.

A shriek tore from her throat as the shark breached the surface almost within touching distance. As it turned on its side she glimpsed a hideous body like a great tree trunk, rust-coloured with huge pectoral fins. The conical head belonged unmistakably to a great white hunter, not for nothing known as the white death.

'Harry, I love you!' she screamed with all her might. They might be her last words but no shark was going to rob her of them, not even the white death itself.

His muscles flexed as he heaved on the oars, his concentration so acute that she wondered if he'd heard her. Then he looked up with a smile which rivalled the coral for luminosity.

She was jolted by a scraping along the side of the boat. At first she thought the shark had attacked them again, then she saw that they were passing over the bar with no time to choose where they crossed. Moments later they were safely inside the coral barrier. The shark's dorsal fin streaked away towards the horizon. Harry had fought the white death and won.

Her fluttering heart felt as if it would leap from her chest as Harry brought them back to the beach. The moment they scraped on to the sand he leapt from the boat and lifted her out bodily, cradling her as if he would never let her go. His heartbeat pounded in time with hers.

His kiss was fiercely possessive, giving her no time to arm herself against the assault on her senses. She tasted salt on his lips, felt the invasion of his tongue, and kissed him back with reckless abandon.

She rested her head against his salt-frosted chest. 'Oh, Harry, I thought we were going to die.'

Like a sleepwalker awakening, he set her down gently and bent to pull the boat higher up the beach.

It was then that she saw how he could interpret her two statements. He thought her declaration was made because she thought they were doomed. Now that they were safe would he still want to hear it?

CHAPTER NINE

LISA was still shaking with reaction when she reached the house, but whether it was with the shock of the shark attack or the sudden violence of Harry's kiss she didn't know.

Although terrified by the shark, she had never doubted that Harry would get them safely back to shore. Where did this crazy belief in his omnipotence come from? He wouldn't welcome it, she was certain.

Just as he didn't welcome her love, she thought bitterly as she slammed into her bedroom and stripped off the sodden jeans. The encounter with the shark had soaked her to the skin. Unwilling to be caught in the shower when Harry returned, she dried herself roughly with a towel and dressed in fresh shorts and a T-shirt.

He was waiting for her when she emerged. As soon as she saw him standing amid the ruins of the kitchen her hand went to her mouth. The shark attack had driven the memory of her frenzied urge to eat from her mind. Now she stared in horror at the chaos she'd caused.

'Like to talk about it?' he asked quietly.

'I was hungry. I made myself something to eat.'

Her defensive tone didn't fool him for a moment.
'It looks more as though the shark was in here in
a feeding frenzy.'

He didn't know how close to the mark he was.
She covered her face with trembling hands. 'I
couldn't stop myself. That's why I had to join you
in the boat, to get away from the temptation.'

Gently but insistently he pried her fingers away
from her face. His grey gaze was soft as he looked
at her. He understood, she realised in amazement.
The most shameful secret she possessed had just
been laid bare before him and he understood!
Wonder flooded through her until she felt luminous with its healing light.

With an arm around her shoulders he steered her
to the couch, dropping to his knees on the floor
beside her. 'How long have you been a compulsive
eater?'

She closed her eyes as a shudder shook her, then
she made herself look at him. He deserved as much.
'Since my early teens,' she confessed in a husky
whisper.

'Was it the insecurity of your upbringing?'

There was no censure in his voice and she basked
in the warmth of his empathy. 'I did some counselling, and it seems that when I was growing up
eating was the only area of my life over which I
had control.'

'So you used it to block out the other parts of
your life which were out of control,' he observed.
Then another thought struck him and he regarded
her with horrified self-condemnation. 'My lord,

when I think of all the things I said to you about your weight when I was working on your father's biography.'

The pain in his voice found an echo inside her. She rushed to assuage it, and her own. 'You mustn't feel badly. You meant to help, and, in a way, you did.'

'By teasing you about something you couldn't help?' His voice was thick with self-disapprobation.

She sat up straighter. 'Don't you see, I *could* help it? I just didn't know it. It took being teased by someone who...whose opinion mattered to me,' her voice dropped at the reminder which he probably wouldn't welcome. 'You made me see that I needed help. My doctor recommended a group where all the members had similar problems. I was finally able to talk out my insecurity instead of eating it out. They taught me other ways to cope and gave me a sense of belonging somewhere for the first time.'

There was a fine sheen across his eyes as he said, 'You poor kid. I never realised how bad it was for you.'

At his description of her she bristled. 'I'm not a kid, Harry. And self-pity was one of the first things I learned to dispense with. It still surfaces occasionally, but not as much as it used to.'

Uncoiling from the floor, he paced to the kitchen and found glasses amid the chaos, pouring cold lemon drinks for them both. He handed one to her, then sat down opposite her, his expression stony.

'I assume it takes a trigger of some kind to set you off again.'

'Probably. It hasn't happened to me for a long time.'

'Until I came along,' he reminded her.

Her hair spun around her head with the force of her denial. 'It wasn't your doing. Don't you see? In the group I learned not to blame anyone else for my problems. I'm the one doing the eating.'

'Which is commendable if not for the fact that you had it under control until I brought you here.'

He was determined to hold himself responsible for her lapse, just as he blamed himself for Kim's death. She remembered accusing him of being a martyr, then wondered if it weren't a perfect excuse to stay uninvolved.

Her spirits sank lower and lower. 'There's no need to sugar-coat it,' she said, her tone defeated. 'You've made no secret about how you feel, so there's no need to blame yourself.'

'It's for your own good,' he went on doggedly.

It was too much. She jumped to her feet, spilling the remains of the drink which was beside her on the floor. 'Then for pity's sake stop doing things for my own good; it's killing me,' she yelled at him and flung herself out of the room.

Dry-eyed, determined not to shed any more tears over Harry Blake, she remained in her room, pretending to herself that she was reading, until a knock came on the door-frame.

'Yes?' she said uninterestedly.

The bamboo curtain moved aside and he stood there. 'I've refuelled the cruiser. It's ready for the trip back to Thursday Island. We can leave first thing tomorrow.'

So that was that. He was taking her back where he had found her and she would probably never see him again. She tried to tell herself it was for the best. She had come to terms with life without him once. She could do it again.

But the aching sense of loss was still with her next morning as she repacked her few clothes into her travel bag. When she came to the sundress she'd worn the day he'd rescued her and they'd made love on the beach she held it against her cheek as memories came flooding back.

He must love her. He had told her so with his body, in every way that a man could. After saving her from the shark he had kissed her with a savagery which betrayed her importance to him. Yet he was letting her go.

Forlornly she folded the dress on top of the rest and added her parents' wedding photo before closing the lid. It felt as if she was closing the door on the best part of her life.

'Ready?'

She looked up to find Harry waiting in the doorway. The sight of him squeezed her heart so hard that she thought she would stop breathing. Moisture from his morning shower glistened on his dark hair like dew on the rain forest canopy.

Dressed for town in tailored beige trousers and a cream pilot's shirt, he looked stunningly handsome.

How would she remember him? Elegantly dressed like this, or heart-stoppingly pagan in torn canvas shorts, his mahogany chest bared, the curling hairs frosted with salt water? Whichever image it was, it was bound to haunt her, she knew as she finished fastening the suitcase. Five long years had taught her that Harry Blake was not an easy man to forget.

'I'm ready,' she said, a hysterical laugh bubbling in her throat at the incongruity of her remark. How could she be ready to do something which was tearing the heart out of her?

'Then let's go.' He picked up her case and she noticed that he was carrying one of his own.

'Are you staying on TI?' she asked, as much for something to say as to hear the answer.

He shook his head. 'I'm coming with you to Cairns.'

'I don't understand.' She thought he couldn't wait to be rid of her. Light slowly dawned. 'It's the story, isn't it? The photo wasn't among the things I brought with me, so you still hope to find it at my flat.'

'Will you let me look for it?'

So it *was* the story. The admission drove the breath out of her as if she'd been punched. 'If I say no you'll probably break in and search the flat anyway.' It was impossible to keep the bitterness out of her voice.

'I suppose I deserved that,' he said.

Yet, she noticed, he didn't deny it. The story *was* the most important thing to him. Oh, he had tried to warn her but she, poor fool, hadn't listened. How many women came up against similar brick walls and thought they were the only ones in the whole world who could change a man?

She remembered reading about a character in a television series, supposedly without any emotions. The actor who played him was said to receive more fan mail than any other actor in the series, mostly from women who thought they could break through his stoic façade and release the emotional man underneath.

It was the greatest of all conceits, the belief that you could change another person, she told herself. If she'd learned nothing else from her support group she had learned that the only person she could change was herself. 'You can look for the photo,' she said on a resigned sigh. 'I doubt if you'll find anything, but you're welcome to try.'

'Thank you. I appreciate it.' But there was no gratitude in his impassive expression. He was probably sorry that he had to travel with her back to Cairns to achieve his aim. Waving her off at the airport would probably suit him better. A tiny glimmer of satisfaction flared inside her at the thought that he wouldn't be rid of her quite so easily.

As they rowed in the dinghy out to the cruiser she realised they would have to go outside the lagoon again. 'What about the shark?' she asked nervously.

'It won't bother us in the larger boat,' he assured her. 'It wasn't a big one in any case.'

To her the gaping mouth with its inward-angled rows of needle-sharp teeth had looked enormous, but perhaps it had been in comparison with the small boat. All the same, she looked around apprehensively for a curving dorsal fin cutting through the water. There was no sign of it as they moved slowly out across the bar and into the deeper water.

The journey back to Thursday Island seemed much shorter than the trip out. Was it because every mile which passed took her further from where she most wanted to be? She found herself thinking yearningly of the honeymoon cave and the magical freshwater spring. If she saw them again it would be in the brisk, businesslike guise of a tour guide.

Her eyes blurred but she blinked hard, determined not to weaken now. She made a mental resolution to be the best tour organiser Harry had ever seen. 'When do you want to start having organised visits to the island?' she asked over the throb of the outboard engines.

He turned away from the steering-wheel. 'Whenever you say we're ready. I trust your judgement on this.'

But not about matters of the heart, she thought bleakly. Aloud she said, 'I'll draw up some plans and mail them to you.'

'You'll need start-up capital,' he said. 'I intend to contribute a substantial share.'

So they were going to be partners in every way except the one which mattered to her. Could she carry it off? Unconsciously her chin lifted and her shoulders straightened. She could and she would, if it killed her.

Harry had booked them on the early-afternoon flight back to Cairns. The plane was a small Fokker Friendship twin turboprop aircraft, which meant that there were only thirty or so other passengers.

They had a three-seat row to themselves. She accepted Harry's offer of the window-seat, unreasonably annoyed when he then took the aisle seat, leaving the middle one vacant. He really couldn't wait to put some distance between them, could he? It was something she should get used to, she supposed.

The rest of the flight passed in a blur. She drank the tea and ate the sandwiches served by the cabin staff, hardly noticing when the red bauxite cliffs of Weipa appeared beneath them. The mining town was the only stop on the flight and they reached Cairns soon after four-thirty.

'Where are you staying in Cairns?' she asked Harry as he loaded their bags into a hire-car. Her flat was only a ten-minute drive from the airport, and he had offered her a lift home.

'I've booked a room at Hides.' He named one of the oldest and most atmospheric of the Cairns hotels.

A pang shot through her. He hadn't even considered staying with her. Yet they were lovers. Unless she had imagined the scene on the beach at Drummer Island. Yet every touch, every movement and every one of her shooting-star responses resonated through her as a kind of cellular reminder.

Even if she forced her mind to do so, her body would never forget him. There was no way she could have imagined a scene of such beauty and passion. Just thinking about it sent waves of heat shimmering through her.

'I'll drop you at your flat, then go on to my hotel,' he said, his tone cool and distant. The island seemed like a long way away.

'Do you want to stay for a meal? I left the freezer fairly well stocked.'

Did he know how reluctant she was to let him go? 'Sounds good,' he agreed.

Then she remembered. He probably wanted to use the time to look around for his precious photo. If he found it it would be the last she would see of him. The certainty took some of the pleasure out of his acceptance of her invitation.

Nevertheless, she found herself wanting to show off her flat. She was particularly proud of having furnished and decorated it stylishly on a limited budget. When she'd bought it the furniture was mostly glass and chrome and the upholstery done in heavy dark velvets. As soon as she could she'd replaced it with lighter fabrics and bamboo furniture, in keeping with the tropical location, just one block back from the waterfront and a short walk from the centre of town.

A decorator friend for whom she'd booked a successful world trip had advised her to use mirrors to make the small rooms seem larger. Then she'd found a superb glass and rattan table with chairs covered in cream French linen at Rusty's Bazaar. Rusty's was a Cairns landmark, where you could buy almost anything. Her collection of oriental prints and scrolls came from the same place.

'I hope you like house-plants,' she told Harry when they started up the staircase to her flat. 'Since I moved in mine have grown to jungle proportions.' Her cordyline now reached the ceiling.

'The rain forest atmosphere will remind me of home,' he said on a laugh. 'How do they survive when you're away travelling?'

'I have most of them in self-watering pots, a travel agent's best friend,' she confessed. About to say more, she had to stifle a cry instead at the sight of her front door standing open.

The chaos inside shocked her to her core. Her precious plants were overturned, the water wells spilling on to the carpet. The linen chair covers had been slashed open, and every print on her walls had been vandalised. She stared at the mess, too stunned to cry.

Harry pushed past her into the room. 'Stay here. I'll make sure the intruders have gone.'

She grasped his arm. 'Be careful.' She didn't know what she would do if anything happened to him.

He gave her a wry look. 'Thanks. I intend to.'

She heard him moving from room to room, opening and shutting doors and cupboards. Finally he returned, his face set. 'Whoever they were, they've gone.'

'Do you think Tyler Thornton could have done it?'

Harry's eyes roved over the chaos. 'Anything's possible, but it isn't really his style. From what I know of Thornton, he hates to get his hands dirty.'

'And he called you from Brisbane,' she remembered. Then she bit her lip. 'I suppose he could have said he was in Brisbane to establish an alibi.'

Harry shook his head. 'Too easy to check with his editor.'

She gave a shaky laugh. 'I must be getting paranoid. It's probably just your everyday burglar who hasn't a clue about any photo.'

'It's possible.' He didn't sound convinced. 'Just in case, don't touch anything until the police have had a look.' Taking his own advice, he wrapped a handkerchief around the telephone handset before making his call.

While they waited for the police she offered him a cold drink from the refrigerator, one of the few items which hadn't been vandalised, although most of the contents looked as if they had been opened and checked.

Perched on kitchen stools, they sat silently sipping their drinks. After a while Harry said, 'Are you sure you're all right, Lisa?'

'I'm fine,' she said determinedly. If she gave way now she would crumble into little pieces. Her control was the thinnest possible veneer. But giving way wouldn't help, and it wouldn't change what had happened.

'This place means a lot to you, doesn't it?'

'It's my base, my security—or it was.' Knowing her family background, he understood how important it was to her to have a secure base, something she'd never enjoyed while she was growing up. Moving from place to place, always looking back over their shoulders, she'd vowed to have her own home as soon as she was an adult.

'You won't stay here now?'

'How can I?' Despite herself, her voice rose on a note of despair.

'It's all right to let go,' Harry suggested, watching her worriedly. 'You don't have to be a hero.'

'I'm not being a hero.' At the same time she was taking food out of the refrigerator and lining it up on the counter-top. When Harry's hand on her wrist stopped the compulsive movement she jerked back as if stung. Her hand went to her mouth. 'Oh, God!'

The tears came then, hot and sharp, and he held her against him, stroking her hair while he murmured meaningless words of comfort. When the worst was over she lifted a tear-stained face up to him. 'It's so awful, Harry. What am I going to do?'

'Go on. We don't have any choice.'

She wondered if he was thinking about Kim. How had he managed to go on after such a tragedy? Finding her home in ruins was devastating, but at least no one had been hurt. 'I feel so—so violated,' she said.

'It's a fairly common reaction when something like this happens,' the police officer explained when she arrived to investigate.

Lisa's sweeping gesture encompassed the chaos around them. 'Why did they have to make such a mess?'

The police officer murmured in sympathy. 'Sometimes the vandalism is harder to take than the loss of personal possessions. At least they can be replaced. Restoring your feeling of safety in your own home takes a lot longer.'

The woman's partner moved to the door, which they'd been careful not to touch. 'No signs of forced entry,' she commented, making notes. Then she turned to Lisa. 'Have you lost a key recently, or given a key to anyone?'

Beside her she felt Harry tense. Was he waiting for her to say she'd given a key to Simon? 'I haven't lost or given a key to anyone,' she said firmly.

'Well, at least you don't have to replace your front door,' the police officer said. 'Do you have the serial numbers of the valuables you've lost?'

'I keep a list, but there doesn't seem to be anything missing.' It had been puzzling Lisa since she'd noticed the fact. Her television, video recorder and compact-disc player were all in plain sight and unharmed.

The police officer chewed her pen thoughtfully. 'That is odd. Maybe it was older teenagers, out for kicks.'

Sick at heart, Lisa turned away. 'I can't believe people would do something like this for kicks.'

The officer's smile was wry. 'You'd be surprised.' She closed the notebook. 'There isn't a lot for us to go on, so don't hold out too much hope that we'll catch the culprit. We'll check for finger-prints, but, with nothing taken, the case is pretty flimsy.'

Lisa wondered whether she should mention the photo, then decided against it. Since she'd never seen the photo and seriously doubted whether it still existed, it would only waste the police's time.

She watched dispiritedly as the officers finished their investigation. Harry slipped an arm around her. 'When they've gone I'll stay and help you clean up.'

The lump in her throat made speech impossible, so she nodded dumbly. She had wanted to delay his departure, but not this way.

After the police left they began the thankless task. Clutching a cushion against her chest, she asked Harry, 'Do you think I should have told the police about the photo?'

'Possibly, but they seemed convinced this was the work of teenagers.'

'It couldn't be the photo, could it? Nobody knows about it but you and me.'

'And Tyler Thornton,' he added pointedly.

'He could have told someone, I suppose.' Sud-denly she hurled the cushion against a wall. 'How could anybody *do* this to me?'

There was admiration in the look Harry gave her. 'Good girl. You'll need a bit of fighting spirit.'

'Who'll need fighting spirit? Good grief!' She looked up to see Simon Fox framed in the doorway, his eyes as round as saucers as he surveyed the damage.

'What happened here?' he asked, stepping gingerly over an upturned footstool.

'As you can see, I had visitors while I was away,' she informed him, her voice metallic with unshed tears. Her fighting spirit was rapidly evaporating. Belatedly she remembered her manners. 'Simon Fox, this is Harry Blake. Harry is an old friend of my family's.'

She noticed his eyebrows arch menacingly at her description of him. Well, let him! The role of Dutch uncle was his choice, not hers.

Simon offered his hand. 'Pleased to meet you.' Under the pleasantry there was a wary edge in his voice.

She compared the two men. Simon's blond good looks made him look like the sun to Harry's shadow as snapping blue eyes appraised steely grey ones. They were almost the same height, but Harry's uneven shoulder and outdoorsman's build made him look more ruggedly masculine alongside Simon's gym-honed muscularity.

Her heart gave a lurch. How could she have thought of Simon as a substitute for Harry? Not sun and shadow, she amended to herself, light and shadow. Simon came across as disappointingly lightweight alongside Harry's dark solidarity.

Simon gave Harry a look of distrust. 'Have you called the police?'

Harry had gone back to work and didn't look up. She answered for him. 'They've just left. The odd part is, nothing of value seems to be missing.'

'Maybe it was a teenage prank,' Simon suggested.

'That's what the police think. Whatever happened to ringing doorbells and running away?'

Simon's arm slid possessively around her shoulders, and she saw Harry look up then away. Discreetly she moved out of Simon's reach. 'Did you come for something special?' she asked him.

He gave Harry a resentful glare. 'Do I need a reason? I wanted to see if you were back yet. I thought maybe we could go out for dinner.'

Considering that she hadn't known she was returning today until Harry had announced that the cruiser was ready, this struck her as odd, but she dismissed it. Simon sometimes dropped in unannounced, on the off-chance that she'd be at home. 'As you can see, I'm not going anywhere for a while,' she said with an apologetic smile.

Simon took his jacket off and hung it from the door-handle, loosening his tie with one hand. 'In that case, I may as well pitch in and help.'

Her sense of disappointment was almost palpable. Distressing as the break-in was, she had taken comfort from knowing it allowed her to spend more precious hours with Harry. 'It's kind of you,' she said, aware of how lame she sounded.

Harry straightened abruptly. 'Since you have your friend here to help, I'll go and check into my hotel. I'll give you a call later and make sure you're all right.'

Harry, don't go. The request came so intensely that at first she thought she'd voiced it aloud, until she recognised it as a silent plea. With a sick feeling she watched Harry dust himself off and pick up his travel bag which stood near the open door. 'Thanks for everything,' she said, aware of how empty the words sounded. Should she thank him for becoming her lover then turning her out of his life?

He swung his bag over his shoulder. 'I'll be in touch. Call me if you need me.'

He meant for anything practical, not for the sake of her aching heart. 'I will,' she said dully.

'Thanks for taking care of Lisa,' Simon said, stepping between her and Harry. The proprietorial sound of it made her stomach clench in protest.

Harry's jaw tightened but he said nothing as he stepped into the hall. The pain of watching him go hit her like a physical blow. Everything in her longed to run after him. If she hadn't known why he was so anxious to be on his way she might have suited the deed to the thought.

But she knew all right. The photo was obviously not to be found, so there was nothing to keep him here. It's over, she thought as a dead feeling settled on her chest. To Harry she was yesterday's news.

CHAPTER TEN

'CHEER up, I'm here.'

Lisa's thin smile didn't reach her eyes as she turned back to find Simon sifting through a pile of debris. 'There's no need to go through those,' she told him. 'I'll probably throw the lot away.'

He continued his careful assessment of the damaged prints. At this rate it would take them all night to clean up one room, she thought crossly.

Something in her manner alerted him. He dropped the prints and came to her, his arms outstretched. 'I've missed you this week.'

He was waiting to hear that she'd missed him, but the words stalled in her throat. In truth the only time she'd given Simon a thought was when she'd wanted to make Harry more aware of her as a woman.

As his arms came around her she tensed involuntarily. His mouth was on her hair and he pulled away, looking down at her in surprise. 'Not even a welcome-home kiss?' He tried again to pull her into his arms.

'Simon, stop, please.' The urgency in her voice finally reached him and he dropped his arms. She took a step back. 'I have something to tell you.'

He wrinkled his brow distastefully. 'It sounds like bad news.'

'Not really, although you might think so at first. I want to hand in my resignation from your employ.'

He folded his arms across his chest, presenting a picture of paternal understanding. 'It's all right, darling, I know what this is about.'

It was her turn to look puzzled. 'You do?'

'It's the burglary. You're tired and overwrought, still in shock if anything. You want to turn and run away from everything familiar.'

'Don't tell me what I feel,' she snapped, annoyed by his arrogance. Why hadn't she spotted his irritating father-knows-best attitude before? 'My decision has nothing to do with the burglary. I'm setting up my own travel agency concentrating on the Torres Strait region.'

'It's a bit sudden, isn't it? If I'd known you were planning to go into competition with me I'd have thought twice about approving your leave.'

A vestige of the friendship she'd felt for him until now surfaced. 'Don't make it hard for me, Simon. The leave was owed to me, as it happens. But I'd rather you didn't pay me for it than regard it as some kind of conspiracy.'

'But it is, isn't it?' he said darkly. 'You go away knowing you're the woman in my life, and come back with "don't touch" signs all over you.' He reached for her and again she recoiled. 'You know how I feel about you, Lisa,' he appealed. 'I want you to be my wife.'

This was the first time he'd mentioned marriage in so many words. Now that she was slipping out of his grasp he was upping the stakes considerably.

He mistook her hesitation for interest. 'You must have known I want to marry you?'

'I didn't know, Simon, and I'm sorry. I thought we were good friends.'

'Only because you insist on keeping things friendly. You know I want more from you.' He moved towards her, his hands sliding around the back of her neck. As he bent his head to kiss her she ducked beneath the circle of his arms.

'I was hoping we could stay friends, but I suppose not,' she said in a small voice. Turning, she opened her hands in a gesture of appeal. 'If you must know, I'm in love with Harry Blake.' There, it was said. The mere mention of his name sent cleansing whispers of air through her soul.

Simon's eyebrows shot up. 'The hot-shot journalist friend of your family?' He gave the last four words a heavy emphasis. 'Isn't he the man who wrote your father's life-story?'

'Yes, among many other books and newspaper articles, but these days he owns Drummer Island. He's thirty-two, a widower and has all his own teeth,' she finished tiredly, wishing Simon would leave. But he hadn't finished with her yet.

'I suppose as well as teaming up with him on his little island you plan to share the spoils from the Russian royalty story?' he asked, a nasty smile turning up the corners of his mouth.

Her head came up in astonishment. 'How do you know about the story?'

He looked smug. 'Tyler Thornton told me. He came to the agency looking for you and we had a few drinks together. More than a few, actually. By the end of the evening he was only too keen to tell me what he was looking for.'

'Did he do this?' Her gesture encompassed the chaos around them.

'He flew back to Brisbane the next day. I haven't seen him since then.'

Something odd in his voice told her that there was more. It came to her in a rush. 'It was you, wasn't it? You were the one who ransacked my flat. You must have taken my spare key from my office drawer—my locked office drawer,' she finished pointedly.

'Sensibly I have keys to every lock in the office,' he informed her. 'If you hadn't returned without warning, I'd have had time to finish here. As it is, there are a few places I haven't looked yet.'

All of which explained his sudden arrival at her flat, and his willingness to help her clean up. 'Why are you doing this?' she asked despairingly.

He seemed almost eager to satisfy her curiosity. 'The photo is worth money, which I happen to need. I thought having the media's little red darling on my staff might turn things around, but last week the bank called in my overdraft. What with the new premises in Cooktown and Townsville, I have to find cash from somewhere.'

'So it was all a lie. I was simply a promotional tool to you all along.' She felt as if someone had snatched a rug out from under her feet.

'I'm surprised you didn't work it out for yourself. I needed a gimmick to put the agency on the map. You were it.'

'But you offered me marriage.' She couldn't believe he would use her to such an extent.

'I meant it, too. The publicity would have been a dream.'

'You're unbelievable,' she gasped as shock piled upon shock. If only she hadn't let Harry leave he could have helped her to deal with this. Added to the destruction of her flat, it was too much. Her head began to spin.

Simon grasped her roughly by the elbow and gave her a slight shake. 'Don't faint on me now, darling. I need you to help finish the search.'

With an effort she collected herself. 'It isn't here. You've looked almost everywhere.'

'Everywhere but among the things you took with you. Come on.' He steered her towards the bedroom, where her travel case stood inside the door.

Alarm shrilled through her. Now that he had no reason to keep up an act Simon's mood was dangerous. For the first time she realised that he might mean her serious harm. She resisted his urging.

Her strength was no match for his. He jerked her across the floor so hard that she stumbled through the bedroom door and fell against the bed. His hooded gaze roved over her sprawled figure. 'Worried that I might take away more than the photo? It's tempting.' She held her breath, then he made a dismissive noise deep in his throat. 'It isn't worth the risk. But if I don't find the photo I might change my mind.'

His threat made her heart pound so loudly that she was sure he must hear it. Afraid to anger him further, she strove to sound calm. 'There's no need for violence, Simon. We know each other. I'll help you if I can, but I'm afraid it's a wild-goose chase.'

'A golden goose is more like it. Nice as it is to have your belated co-operation, I think I can manage alone.'

He unzipped her travel bag and began pulling her things out of it, barely glancing at the articles of clothing as they fell to the floor.

'I've already searched the bag. There's nothing there,' she said when she could stand it no longer.

'You'd make a lousy Customs officer.' He took out a pocket knife and snapped it open. The sight of the gleaming blade sent waves of nausea through her. He ripped the lining of the bag, searching every inch of it. With a curse he threw the remnants aside and looked around. 'It has to be here; I can feel it.'

'You've already looked everywhere.'

'There's still one possibility.' His eyes gleamed fanatically as he picked up her parents' wedding photo from the floor. A moment ago he'd discarded it without a glance.

Tendrils of rage coiled through her and she launched herself at him, reaching for the photo with desperate fingers. He mustn't be allowed to contaminate the most precious memento she had of her parents. 'Leave that alone,' she screamed, her nails raking at his face.

He fended her off effortlessly, holding the photo aloft with his free hand. 'This is important to you, is it?'

'It's all I have to remind me of my parents. Give it to me.'

'Get out of my way.' With a mighty shove he bowled her backwards on to the bed and raised the photo high. The glass smashed against the edge of her dresser and her parents' photo tumbled to the floor. He paid it no heed, more intent on a sepia-coloured photograph which had been wedged behind the first. 'What have we here?'

As he tore the photo out and dropped the frame alongside her on the bed, she saw that it was the picture Harry had described to her.

'It was there all the time.' No wonder her mother had so carefully bequeathed Lisa the wedding photo. She had treasured it for its own sake, not suspecting that the antique frame concealed a secret.

'What a surprise,' Simon said nastily, sounding as if he didn't believe her. He grabbed her wrist and pulled her upright.

Her wrist burned as she attempted to twist free. 'You've got what you want—let me go.'

'Let her go, Fox, now!'

The command crackled through the air as Harry barrelled through the open bedroom door. He looked like a man possessed.

Fear for him gripped her. 'Harry, he's got a knife,' she cried.

Harry's eyes shifted briefly to her then scorched Simon again. 'Knife or no knife, if he doesn't let you go I'll tear him apart with my bare hands, so help me.'

'Who needs her? I've got what I wanted.' Simon thrust her against Harry, almost bowling them both over. Automatically Harry's arms closed around her and she clung to him, revelling in the strength of his hold and the reassuring aura of his presence. Harry glanced down at her.

'Are you all right?'

'Yes; he didn't touch me.'

'It wouldn't pay him.' He turned his attention to Simon. 'You may as well give up. The police are on their way.'

For the first time Simon's arrogance faltered. 'How did you know?'

'You're the only one with access to Lisa's keys and contact with Tyler Thornton. A phone call to a finance editor friend of mine confirmed that your agency's in financial trouble. It all adds up.'

With a savage cry Simon held the photo high. In his other hand he held a cigarette lighter, which he ignited. The flame hovered a hair's breadth from the photo. 'Either I walk out of here or this goes up in smoke.'

Her panic-stricken gaze flew from Simon to Harry. She knew how badly Harry wanted the photo. Her heart ached for him.

'Burn it.'

Simon looked as startled as she felt. 'What did you say?'

'I said burn it, Fox. I don't give a damn.'

His arm tightened around her as tears stung the backs of her eyes. How could Harry sacrifice something so important to him? Unless he hoped to bluff Simon into surrendering.

She held her breath as the flames licked at the photo, but Harry remained carved out of granite. The heat of his muscles inflamed her senses and she wondered if he knew that he was holding her tightly enough to snap her in two. Somehow it felt good. She was safe at last.

Sirens rent the air around them and pounding footsteps approached the flat. Two police officers shouldered her and Harry aside to get to Simon. 'Is this the man?'

'That's him.' The ice in Harry's voice chilled Lisa until she remembered what he'd just done to Harry. The remains of the photo smouldered on the floor. One of the officers stamped it out.

What followed was a confusing blur of interviews, statements and gathering the charred photo remains as evidence. Lisa thought it would never end. At last the police pronounced themselves satisfied and left. Simon had already been taken away under arrest.

The silence in the ruined flat was deafening. She slumped on to a slashed chair and rested her head in her hands. 'I can't take much more of this.'

Harry's hands dropped to her shoulders and he massaged them gently, easing her tension. 'You

won't have to. It's over now.' Irresistibly he urged
her to her feet, supporting her all the while. 'Come
on, we're getting out of here.'

'But I've nowhere else to go. I suppose a hotel...'

His look was amused and affectionate. 'Do you
always talk so much when you're being rescued?'

'Am I? Being rescued, I mean?'

'Leave it to me.'

They must be four of the sweetest words in the
English language, she thought as he guided her out
of the flat and locked it behind them. Downstairs
his rental car waited, and he opened the passenger-
door for her. 'Get in.'

'But where are we...? Sorry.' Her barrage of
questions tailed off when she saw his impatient
frown. She was talking too much again.

She made herself relax as he drove off. There
would be time later to tell him how sorry she was
that the photo had been destroyed. Knowing how
much it meant to him, she wondered at his
calmness.

Wherever he was taking her, she was safe; that
much she knew. She decided to sit back and enjoy
being rescued. At least it gave her the gift of a little
longer in his company.

Twilight bathed the landscape in gold as they
drove out of town along the Kennedy Highway. She
recognised Smithfield, although they didn't stop at
the famous Henry Ross look-out. The road wound
through steep hills clad in dark rain forest which
enclosed them as if they were driving through a
tunnel.

'We're going to Kuranda!' she exclaimed in sudden realisation. 'I haven't been there since Mama and Papa died.'

'I have a house up there,' he explained. 'I was only staying at Hides for convenience.'

Until he knew whether the photo was to be found, she thought dismally. She pushed the thought away. What was done was done. 'We lived there for two years,' she said, unaware of the gladness which coloured her voice at the memory. 'It was the longest we ever stayed in one place. I really felt at home there.'

He glanced at her, then back to the winding road. 'Why did you sell the house, then?'

'Papa left me no choice. In his will he stipulated that the house was to be sold and I was to have the proceeds, which I used to buy my flat and make a few small investments.'

'Maybe your father was afraid you'd become a recluse, alone in the rain forest,' Harry observed.

She sighed. 'He was probably right. But I still miss it. From the front veranda you could see all the way across the Barron Gorge.'

Ten minutes later he pulled up in Kuranda and she could hardly believe her eyes. 'It's our house! Don't tell me *you* bought it? Oh, Harry, how wonderful. But how did you manage it?'

Her delight sparked an answering light in his steely gaze. 'When I saw it advertised I sent a proxy to the auction. Maybe part of me hoped that one day I could bring you back here.'

Almost overcome, she bit back the tears of joy which threatened to overflow. 'What a lovely thought. Oh!'

Her cry of surprise was prompted when Harry swept her into his arms and carried her across the wooden veranda, fumbling the door open before carrying her over the threshold.

Inside, she gave him a shy smile. 'I thought you only did that with your bride.'

For once Harry's silver tongue seemed to desert him. 'You do,' he said at last.

Uncertainty descended on her like a cloud. 'Harry?'

'I guess in my own way I'm trying to propose to you,' he said gruffly.

'You want to marry me?'

'If you'll have me.'

She could hardly speak for the lump which rose in her throat as large as an apple. Around it, she gasped, 'Of course I'll have you, Harry Blake. I've never wanted any other man since the day we met.'

'Not even Simon Fox?'

'Simon was never my lover, Harry, you must believe me. Today I found out that I was only a marketing tool to him.'

Closing the door to shut out the night, he opened his arms. 'Why are we standing here discussing Simon Fox?'

Because there was so much she wanted to say and she didn't know where to start. His arms seemed like the best possible place. When they enfolded her his embrace was like a homecoming, and she sighed, nestling against him. 'I do love you, more than anything in the world.'

His lips grazed her hair. 'I love you, too. The thought of anyone harming you makes me murderously angry.'

'Which was how you looked when you stormed into my flat today,' she murmured. 'I thought you were going to kill Simon.'

His fingers flexed against her back. 'I wanted to.'

Her uncertain gaze went to his face. In the gathering dark the planes and angles looked forbidding, until she saw the warmth which gleamed in his eyes. 'But marriage, Harry. Are you sure? What about what happened to Kim?'

He gave a hollow laugh and stroked her hair possessively. 'Staying away from you was supposed to keep you from harm. It didn't work too well, did it?'

'I suppose not.'

The stroking continued all the way down the side of her face to her throat until eddies of pleasure began to spiral through her. 'So I've decided the best way to take care of you is to keep you under my eye.'

'It sounds like heaven to me. But what about the photo?'

Tiny kisses feathered her forehead. 'I thought I made it clear that your safety was what mattered. I said I don't care about the photo and I mean it.'

She meant more to him than his story. The awareness made her giddy with satisfaction, until a worry-frown etched itself into her brow. 'What will happen to your book?'

'I'm giving up non-fiction as of now. No more investigating controversial subjects which could put you at risk.'

When she made a murmur of protest he added, 'I shan't give up writing altogether. Without the photo there's no proof that your aunt was Lyudmila Duskov, so it won't work as non-fiction. But I *can* write the story of the two sisters as a novel. It might even be more fun that way.'

'My husband, the best-selling author,' she experimented. 'It sounds wonderful.'

He cupped her chin in one hand and brought her face up, his eyes dark. 'Which part?'

Her eyelashes feathered her cheeks as she shielded her suddenly shy gaze from him. 'Can't you guess?'

'I think so.' His hand slid to the nape of her neck and he crushed her mouth against his. The hunger in his kiss resonated through her until she parted her lips in eager response, thrilling to the crashing chords of ecstasy playing through every part of her.

Rocked tightly against him, she became aware of his urgent need for her and knew a thrill of pride. He wanted her, now and forever. A river of molten lava poured through her, filling every crevice with an answering desire as bright and powerful as an explosion of shooting stars.

When he led her to his bedroom it seemed somehow symbolic that it should have been the room her parents had shared. The furniture was new, of course, the bed a king-sized water-bed covered in downy grey velvet. It teased her skin when he settled her against it.

The rippling movement beneath her made her eyes widen. 'I've never made love on a water-bed,' she confessed in a hesitant whisper.

His smile radiated love. 'Want to know something? Neither have I.'

Knowing that she was the only woman he'd ever brought here made the moment special beyond her wildest dreams. 'I do love you.' she repeated, knowing she would never tire of saying it or being told that he loved her in return.

His shirt dropped to the floor and he stretched out beside her, his chest hard and warm against her side. His fingers worked the buttons of her shirt until it fell open and he could kiss her breasts until she cried his name in feverish abandon.

He mastered his own needs in order to make slow, exquisite love to her until she cried aloud with the beauty of it. When his passion could no longer be bridled she was more than ready to journey with him to the edge of the world and back, her cries of release mingling with his husky words of love. It was an ending and a beginning, and her heart overflowed with joy.

Much later he brought a tray to their bedside. The champagne glasses she recognised, but not the food. When he pressed a piece against her lips she understood. 'The wongai fruit! It has a lot to answer for.'

He grinned. 'Remind me never to feed them to the tourists. If they're always this effective we'll never get them to go home.'

Her sigh of contentment rippled between them. 'Right now I feel so good that I don't care if they all stay.'

'Not all the time,' he cautioned. 'We'll need some privacy.'

'Quite a lot of it, if tonight's any guide,' she mused.

'You're not sorry you agreed to marry me?'

She chewed her lip. 'Never, although second marriages can be a challenge.'

He frowned. 'You mean Kim and me?'

'No, you and me. Remember, as far as Alf Nawi and his people are concerned, we're already married. We did spend a night in the cave of lovers.'

He dropped a kiss on the end of her nose. 'Then the sooner we make it official, the better.'

Her smile lit up the room. 'I thought we just did.'

As he took the champagne glass from her fingers his eyes gleamed with a fire that she was sure she would come to know intimately in the future. When he opened his arms she went into them willingly, the sense of homecoming making her want to cry with happiness. 'That was just for practice,' he said. 'Every good marriage starts with a rehearsal.'

And she had no doubt that theirs would be a very good marriage indeed.

AUSTRALIA
READER SURVEY 1992

Spare a few minutes to tell us your views about our selection of Romances set in Australia and we will send you a FREE Mills & Boon Romance as our thank you. Don't forget to fill in your name and address, so that we know where to send your FREE book!

Please tick the appropriate box to indicate your answer ☑

1   From where did you obtain your 'Australia' gift pack?

Mills & Boon Reader Service ☐

WH Smiths, John Menzies, other Newsagents ☐

Boots, Woolworth, Department Stores ☐

Supermarket ☐

Received as a gift ☐

Other (please specify) _____

2   If the pack was a gift, who bought it for you? _____

3   If you bought the pack for yourself, why did you choose it? _____

_____

4   Did you enjoy the Australian settings of the books in this pack?

Very Much ☐   Not Very Much ☐

Quite a Lot ☐   Not At All ☐

What did you like about the design of the pack? _____

_____

What did you dislike about the design of the pack? _____

_____

Are there any other settings or themes you think would work well in a collection of stories? e.g. These could be different countries, but could also include a season or special date in the calendar, or an event.

_____

Have you bought, or received any other Mills & Boon Gift packs?

Mother's Day Pack ☐   Intimate Moments Pack ☐

New Author Pack ☐   Romance Christmas Pack ☐

Holiday/Summer Pack ☐   Temptation Christmas Pack ☐

9 How many Mills & Boon Romances do you usually read in a month?

Less than one a month ☐   Five to ten a month ☐

One a month ☐   More than ten a month ☐

Two to four a month ☐   Other (please specify) _____

10 If this is the first time you have read a Mills & Boon Romance, do you intend to purchase more of them?

Yes ☐   Not sure ☐

No ☐

11 Which of the following series do you read?

Mills & Boon: Silhouette:

Romance ☐   Sensation ☐

Best Seller ☐   Special Edition ☐

Temptation ☐   Desire ☐

Medical Romance ☐   Loveswept ☐

Masquerade ☐   Zebra ☐

Collection ☐

12 What age group are you?

−24 ☐   35-44 ☐   55-64 ☐

25-34 ☐   45-54 ☐   65+ ☐

13 Are you a Reader Service subscriber?   Yes ☐   No ☐

If yes, what is your subscription number? _____

Please send your completed form to:

Mills & Boon Reader Service,

FREEPOST, P.O. Box 236, Croydon, Surrey CR9 9EL

THANK YOU FOR YOUR HELP

NO
STAMP
NEEDED

Ms/Mrs/Miss/Mr _____ AU2

Address _____

_____

_____ Postcode _____

_____

You may be mailed with offers from other reputable companies as a result of this appication. Please tick if you would prefer not to receive such offers ☐

4 FREE

Romances
and 2 FREE gifts
just for you!

You can enjoy all the
heartwarming emotion of true love for FREE!
Discover the heartbreak and the happiness, the emotion
and the tenderness of the modern relationships in
Mills & Boon Romances.

We'll send you 4 captivating Romances as a special offer
from Mills & Boon Reader Service, along with the chance to
have 6 Romances delivered to your door each month.

Claim your FREE books and gifts overleaf...

An irresistible offer from Mills & Boon

Here's a personal invitation from Mills & Boon Reader Service, to become a regular reader of Romances. To welcome you, we'd like you to have 4 books, a CUDDLY TEDDY and a special MYSTERY GIFT absolutely FREE.

Then you could look forward each month to receiving 6 brand new Romances, delivered to your door, postage and packing free! Plus our free newsletter featuring author news, competitions, special offers and much more.

This invitation comes with no strings attached. You may cancel or suspend your subscription at any time, and still keep your free books and gifts.

It's so easy. Send no money now. Simply fill in the coupon below and post it to -
Reader Service, FREEPOST, PO Box 236, Croydon, Surrey CR9 9EL.

NO STAMP REQUIRED

Free Books Coupon

Yes! Please rush me my 4 free Romances and 2 free gifts! Please also reserve me a Reader Service subscription. If I decide to subscribe I can look forward to receiving 6 brand new Romances each month for just £9.60, postage and packing free. If I choose not to subscribe I shall write to you within 10 days - I can keep the books and gifts whatever I decide. I may cancel or suspend my subscription at any time. I am over 18 years of age.

Name Mrs/Miss/Ms/Mr _____ EP18R

Address _____

_____

Postcode_____ Signature _____

Offer expires 31st May 1992. The right is reserved to refuse an application and change the terms of this offer. Readers overseas and in Eire please send for details. Southern Africa write to Book Services International Ltd, P.O. Box 41654, Craighall, Transvaal 2024. You may be mailed with offers from other reputable companies as a result of this application. If you would prefer not to share in this opportunity, please tick box. ☐

mps
MAILING
PREFERENCE
SERVICE